WORLD'S OLDEST LIVING DRAGON

By Kate McMullan

Illustrated by Bill Basso

GROSSET & DUNLAP

For the one-and-only Donn Nelson—K.M.

GROSSET & DUNLAP
Published by the Penguin Group
Penguin Group (USA) Inc., 375 Hudson Street, New York, New York 10014, U.S.A.
Penguin Group (Canada), 90 Eglinton Avenue East, Suite 700, Toronto, Ontario,
Canada M4P 2Y3 (a division of Pearson Penguin Canada Inc.)
Penguin Books Ltd, 80 Strand, London WC2R 0RL, England
Penguin Ireland, 25 St Stephen's Green, Dublin 2, Ireland
(a division of Penguin Books Ltd)
Penguin Group (Australia), 250 Camberwell Road, Camberwell,
Victoria 3124, Australia
(a division of Pearson Australia Group Pty Ltd)
Penguin Books India Pvt Ltd, 11 Community Centre, Panchsheel Park,
New Delhi—110 017, India
Penguin Group (NZ), Cnr Airborne and Rosedale Roads, Albany,
Auckland 1310, New Zealand
(a division of Pearson New Zealand Ltd)
Penguin Books (South Africa) (Pty) Ltd, 24 Sturdee Avenue, Rosebank,
Johannesburg 2196, South Africa

Penguin Books Ltd, Registered Offices:
80 Strand, London WC2R 0RL, England

Text copyright © 2006 by Kate McMullan. Illustrations copyright © 2006 by Bill
Basso. All rights reserved. Published by Grosset & Dunlap, a division of Penguin
Young Readers Group, 345 Hudson Street, New York, New York 10014. DRAGON
SLAYERS' ACADEMY and GROSSET & DUNLAP are trademarks of Penguin
Group (USA) Inc. Printed in the U.S.A.

Library of Congress Control Number: 2005026886

ISBN 0-448-44112-8   10 9 8 7

Chapter I

Wiglaf slurped the eel soup that Frypot had overcooked for lunch. It wasn't as foul-tasting as his mother's cabbage soup, but it was a close second.

Erica carried her tray over to the Class I table. She looked glum.

"What's wrong?" Wiglaf asked as she sat down next to him.

"The new Sir Lancelot Catalog still hasn't come," she said. "It should have been here weeks ago." She sighed. "I've been saving up to buy another copy of *The Way of the Knight*. My old copy is totally worn-out."

Just then, Lady Lobelia, clad in a gown of robin's-egg blue, clinked her spoon on her goblet.

She stood up at her place at the head table. "I have an announcement!" she said.

The lads and lasses stopped whining about the food to listen.

"There is more to life than hacking and whacking, lads and lasses," Lady Lobelia said. "There's also community service."

"Uh-oh," said Angus. He had gobbled up his eel soup, and was eyeing Wiglaf's bowl. "Sounds like more work."

"But good work," put in Erica. "We future dragon slayers must always help the less fortunate."

Wiglaf shoved his soup over to the ever-hungry Angus. He glanced at Erica. It was just this sort of goody-goody talk that helped her keep the Future Dragon Slayer of the Month medal pinned to her DSA tunic month after month.

"At my old school," said Janice, "we knitted foot warmers for retired executioners."

"Every week," Lobelia continued, "a group of students will visit Ye Olde Home for Aged

Knights. I'll send the first group this afternoon."

"Ye Olde Home is right outside Toenail!" exclaimed Torblad, who, as it happened, came from the village of Toenail.

"You can ask the aged knights about their glory days," Lobelia went on. "Who knows? They may give you some valuable tips on dragon slaying."

"And on grabbing dragon gold!" added DSA headmaster Mordred. He sat beside his sister Lobelia at the head table. "Don't forget the gold."

"My Gramps used to live at Ye Olde Home," Janice told the others at the Class I table. "But when Daddy struck it rich, he moved Gramps to Golden Years Palace. It's very fancy. Fair damsels take Gramps for walks in the garden. And he has his own jester who juggles and tells him jokes."

Baldrick wiped his nose on his sleeve and raised his hand. "Do we have to go to Ye Olde Home?" he asked.

"Of course not," said Lady Lobelia. "You can

stay here and scrub pots."

"I *want* to go!" said Janice. "Something *wild* will happen. It always does."

Lobelia chose Janice, Erica, Angus, and Wiglaf for the first group. She handed Wiglaf a map. Right after lunch, the four set off for Ye Olde Home.

"I know it's not nice to say," said Angus as they headed north on Huntsman's Path, "but old geezers scare me."

"Why?" asked Wiglaf. "Geezers were young once, just like us."

"That's what's scary!" wailed Angus. "I don't want to get old and shaky and have bad teeth and drool on my tunic!"

"My grandpa never drools on his tunic," said Janice. She popped a piece of gum into her mouth.

"No?" said Angus.

"No," said Janice. "He wears a bib."

"See what I mean?" cried Angus. "It's awful, getting old."

"That's why we are going," said Erica. "Our fresh young faces will bring cheer into the old knights' dreary lives. And what joy I will bring when I recite the poem I wrote about Sir Lancelot. It is long," she added. "But I memorized the whole poem."

When they reached Toenail, Wiglaf looked at Lobelia's map. "We must head that way," he said, pointing east.

As they turned toward the Swamp River, Wiglaf spied a gray stone castle sitting atop a hill. They drew close and Wiglaf saw dozens of rocking chairs sitting on the lawn in front of the castle. Letters carved into the stone above the door read: YE OLDE HOME FOR AGED KNIGHTS.

Erica led the way over the drawbridge. She yanked the bell pull. A minute later, the big wooden front door swung open. And there stood a tall, broad-shouldered man with wavy brown hair and eyes of cornflower blue. He wore a bright red tunic and red leather boots. A patch sewn onto his

tunic spelled out his name: Donn.

"*Buenos días!*" Donn said. "Good day!" He bowed. "Can I help you?"

"We're from Dragon Slayers' Academy," Erica said. "Lady Lobelia sent us."

"Ah, *Señorita* L.!" Donn clasped his hands to his chest. "No fairer damsel ever set slipper upon this earth."

"Yuck," muttered Angus. "I hope he isn't Auntie Lobelia's new boyfriend."

"Welcome to Ye Olde Home," Donn said. "Come in!" He led them inside to a great hall. A fire burned in a big stone fireplace. Flags with faded coats of arms flew from poles above their heads.

Everywhere Wiglaf looked, he saw aged knights. Some wore tunics and breeches. Some wore odd pieces of their old armor. But most sat around in their jammies.

"Talk to the aged knights," said Donn. "They will enjoy—*Ay, caramba!*" he cried suddenly. "Sir

Dribblechin's lost his teeth again. Pardon me."
He hurried off to help him.

The DSA students walked over to two aged knights playing cards.

"Have you any knaves?" said one aged knight to the other.

"Ha-ha—no!" cackled the second. "Go fishing for it!"

The first aged knight drew a card from the pile.

"'Tis a knave!" he cried, showing his card. "I get another turn!"

"That's no knave," said the second aged knight. "That's a jester."

"Same thing," said the first.

"'Tis not!" cried the second.

"'Tis, too!" cried the first.

The aged knights kept arguing. They didn't seem to notice the DSA students.

"Look," whispered Janice, pointing to a group of knights sitting around a large table. "They're playing dragon bingo."

The DSA students headed for the round table. Each knight had a parchment card in front of him. The cards were dotted with small flat stones. Letters at the top of the cards spelled out: D-R-A-G-O-N.

Wiglaf noticed that one of the knights wasn't nearly as aged as the others. He had plump cheeks, dark shoulder-length hair, and a potbelly. He wore faded blue pj's. Wiglaf watched as the plump knight picked up a silvery napkin ring that lay on the table and gazed into it as if it were a mirror. He plucked a gray hair from his head. Then he smiled at his reflection.

Wiglaf thought he had seen this knight somewhere before. But where?

"*Bueno!*" said Donn, coming over to the big round table. "Where were we?" He picked a tile from a box and called, "*Numero* G-32."

All the aged knights who had G-32 on their cards covered it with a stone.

Wiglaf nudged Erica. "Look at the chubby

knight in the blue jammies," he whispered. "Does he look familiar?"

"Where?" said Erica, looking around the room.

Donn reached into the box and took another tile.

"*Numero* N-5," he called. "N-5."

A short, bald knight clutching a cane in one hand called out, "Dragon!"

"That's the only way you'll ever get a dragon again, Roger," cried a skinny, hunched-over knight with poofs of curly white hair. "On a game card!"

All the knights at the bingo table cracked up.

"Stuff a sock in it, Poodleduff!" cried Sir Roger, waving his cane in the air. "I've got 'dragon,' I tell you!"

"Pooh, Roger," said Sir Poodleduff. "You cheated!"

"I never cheat!" cried Sir Roger. "Except in emergencies."

"*Por favor!*" said Donn. "Please! No fighting!"

Sir Roger read back the letters and numbers

on his card.

"*Bueno!*" cried Donn when he finished. "You win, Sir Roger!"

"All right!" said Sir Roger. "What's the prize?"

"An autographed drawing of Sir Lancelot!" said Donn, handing it to him.

"Zounds!" cried Erica. "I wish I had won that!"

But Sir Roger rolled his eyes as he took it.

"Some prize," he muttered. "A picture of a has-been."

Erica gasped. "Sir Lancelot? A has-been?" She turned to Wiglaf. "What can he mean?"

Wiglaf only shrugged.

"And look!" cried Sir Roger. "It's not a real autograph. Even I can see that! Lancelot's name has been rubber-stamped on the drawing. Fie!" He thrust it at Sir Poodleduff. "Here, you take it."

"I don't want it!" cried Sir Poodleduff.

"*Por favor!*" cried Donn. "Stop fighting!"

"Yes, stop!" cried Erica. She stepped forward. "Sir Lancelot is a perfect knight. He is my hero."

"He was a hero once," said Sir Roger.

"But not anymore," said Sir Poodleduff.

"Of course he is!" cried Erica. "Get your ear horns ready, aged knights. You shall hear the poem I have written about Sir Lancelot." Her words rang out:

> *"Many knights are good knights,*
> *Though some few knights are not,*
> *But one knight shines above the rest,*
> *Ne'er will he be forgot."*

As Erica recited, Wiglaf noticed the plump knight's cheeks growing red.

> *"For this knight is the bravest knight*
> *In all of Camelot,*
> *The one, the only perfect knight,*
> *The good Sir Lancelot."*

"Pooh!" called Sir Poodleduff.

"Hear this poem," called Sir Roger.

"He eats a lot, Sir Lancelot!
And then he splits his pants a lot!"

All the aged knights roared with laughter.

Wiglaf saw that the plump knight was slouching way down in his chair. He looked as if he were trying to hide. Now Wiglaf was sure he had seen this knight before.

"Fine!" Erica shouted over the jeering. Her face was red. She looked angry. "I shall stop. But 'tis true. Sir Lancelot *is* a perfect knight."

A smile crept onto the dark-haired knight's face.

Wiglaf gave a sudden gasp. He grabbed Erica's arm.

"That chubby knight," he whispered. "He looks like Sir Lancelot!"

Chapter 2

rica stared at the chubby knight.

"You're right, Wiggie," she said at last. "Yet Sir Lancelot never wrote a word in his autobiography, *A Knight Like I,* about any overweight relative."

Donn tooted on a silver whistle. *"Bueno, señores!"* he called. "Snack time!"

Angus perked up. "Think we get a snack, too?"

Waiters began bringing in silver bowls of salted nuts and goblets of juice.

The chubby knight waved the waiters over. "Bowl of nuts—right here!"

While the snack was being served, Erica rushed over to the chubby knight. Wiglaf and the others were right behind her.

"Sir!" Erica said. "I have had the honor of

meeting Sir Lancelot in person. And, except for an extra fifty pounds, you look very like him. Are you perhaps his cousin?"

"Nay," said the knight, his chubby cheeks reddening. "I am Lancelot."

Erica's mouth dropped open. "YOU are my hero, Sir Lancelot of the Lake?"

The knight raised his silver juice goblet and gazed at his reflection. "Yes, I am Lancelot," he said. "But my hero days are over."

"Oh, sir! What happened? Tell us, please." Erica plopped down on the floor in front of Sir Lancelot.

The other DSA students sat down in front of Sir Lancelot, too.

"All right, you shall hear my tale," said Sir Lancelot, brushing his hair back from his chubby cheeks. "For many years, I slew more wicked dragons than any other knight. I rescued more damsels. I fought the vilest villains. I was the best."

"A perfect knight," Erica sighed.

"Yes." Sir Lancelot nodded in agreement. "But after a time, younger knights began nipping at my heels. One day as I was about to slay a wicked dragon, young Sir Gladblade came charging by and thrust in his sword first!"

"No!" said Erica.

"Yes," said Sir Lancelot. "And that was only the beginning. The next week, as I was getting ready to rescue Lady Pink-Glove from a troll, young Sir Ironspur jumped in and saved her."

"I'll bet she could have handled that troll herself," Janice muttered.

"Not long after that, I threw a vile villain into a dungeon," said Sir Lancelot. "The very next day, young Sir Silverboot fought two vile villains at once, and threw them both into a dungeon."

"Zounds!" exclaimed Angus. "I should have liked to have seen that."

Erica elbowed him sharply.

"What did you do then, sir?" asked Wiglaf.

"Why, I quit," said Sir Lancelot.

"You *quit?*" cried Erica. "You, sir? Oh, say it's not so!"

"'Tis true." Sir Lancelot nodded. "When you have been a perfect knight, it is hard to be anything less." He reached into the bowl of salted nuts and tossed a handful into his mouth. "Instead of getting up at dawn," he went on, chewing, "I started sleeping late and going fishing in the lake. I took up weaving. You should see the lovely flowery tapestries I made."

"Weaving?" Erica looked stricken.

Sir Lancelot nodded. "I spent afternoons in my hammock, reading mysteries. And every night, I feasted. Life was fine until my catalog company went out of business."

"So that's why my catalog never came!" cried Erica.

"Sorry, lass," said Sir Lancelot. "You see, my evil twin brother, Leon, began making Sir Lancelot knock-offs."

"You mean fakes?" said Wiglaf.

"Fakes." Sir Lancelot nodded. " '*Sir Lancelittle,*' he calls them. Sir Lancelittle tool belts. Sir Lancelittle armor. It's junk, but most villagers can't tell the difference." He tossed back some more nuts. "The cheap stuff sells. My catalog business went belly-up. Soon I couldn't pay my servants. I had to move out of my palace. By that time, I'd gained so much weight that my steed couldn't carry me anymore. So I walked here, to Ye Olde Home, and begged to be taken in."

"That's terrible!" cried Erica.

"Totally!" cried Janice, snapping her gum loudly.

"Awful!" said Angus.

Wiglaf shook his head. Sir Lancelot wasn't old. It was wrong for him to be busting out of his pajamas at a home for aged knights.

"But you are a living legend, sir!" cried Erica. "When the going gets tough, I often think, *What would Sir Lancelot do?*"

"Take a long nap," said Sir Lancelot. "That's

what I do most afternoons."

"Listen, good sir!" cried Erica. "*This* is what my hero, Sir Lancelot, is like:

> *When a dragon must be slain,*
> *He always leads the quest.*
> *Of all the many good knights,*
> *Sir Lancelot is best.*"

"Yes, well, that was then." Sir Lancelot shrugged. "Fret not, lass. I am happy here."

"But sir," said Erica. "Do you not want to be the best?"

"Here, I *am* the best, without even trying," said Sir Lancelot. "I'm the only one who can do ten jumping jacks in a row. And I have all my own teeth."

"My hero Sir Lancelot always tried his best," Erica muttered.

If Sir Lancelot heard her, he pretended not to.

On their way back to DSA, Janice picked up a piece of parchment lying in the path. She began reading it.

Erica was very glum as she went. She kept saying, "I can't believe it!"

"I can't believe *this*," Janice said suddenly, stopping in her tracks. "A dragon is in the neighborhood."

Wiglaf and the others stood on tiptoe and read over her shoulder:

I, GRIZZLEGORE,
THE WORLD'S OLDEST LIVING DRAGON,
HAVE MOVED TO A CAVE NEAR YOUR SCHOOL.
I'LL BE STOPPING BY
FOR A NEIGHBORLY VISIT SOON.
HERE'S MY SCHEDULE:
DRAGON WHACKERS ALTERNATIVE SCHOOL—ST. HELGA'S DAY
KNIGHTS 'R' US—ST. BART'S MOTHER'S SISTER'S EVE
PRINCESS PREP—ST. TRIFFID'S BAKE-A-PIE DAY
KNIGHTS NOBLE CONSERVATORY—SPRING FLING WEEKEND

DRAGON STABBERS PREPARATORY—JOHANN THE PEDDLER'S DAY
DRAGON SLAYERS' ACADEMY—APRIL FOOLS' DAY
WHEN I ARRIVE, HAND OVER
ALL YOUR GOLD,
OR SEE YOUR SCHOOL GO UP IN FLAMES.
YOUR FAVORITE FIRE-BREATHER,
GRIZZLEGORE, W.O.L.D.

"He is planning to hit DSA!" Wiglaf cried.
"We must show this to Mordred."

They started running. They came upon
another copy of Grizzlegore's schedule. And
another. The whole path was littered with them.

"The dragon must have dropped them all
over the neighborhood," Angus said, panting.

Back at school, they found the headmaster
in his office. Janice handed him the parchment.
As Mordred read, Wiglaf saw his face go purple
with rage.

"Mordred looks like he might explode,"
whispered Janice. "My Uncle Giles exploded.

Boy, was that ever a mess."

Wiglaf tried not to think about Janice's exploding uncle.

Mordred wadded the parchment into a ball and threw it to the floor. "Threaten to burn down my school, do you, Grizzlegore?" he cried. "Well, go ahead. But you're not getting your claws on any of *my* precious gold."

"Good sir!" cried Wiglaf. "What are you saying?"

"I'm saying no to Grizzlegore, that's what I'm saying!" shouted Mordred, still purple as a plum. "No gold, no how. DSA—up in flames? Pity. But all good things must come to an end. I'm packing up and getting out of here." He began tossing items on his desk into a bag.

"Don't let our school go up in flames, Uncle!" cried Angus. "Please! Give the dragon some gold!"

"Nephew!" barked Mordred. "Bite your tongue!"

The four left Mordred to his packing and headed for the dining hall.

Angus shook his head. "I knew Uncle Mordred was greedy," he said, "but I didn't know he was *this* greedy."

"We can't let a dragon burn down our school," said Janice.

"You're right, Janice," said Erica. "It's up to us to save DSA."

"Maybe Grizzlegore is all bluster," said Angus. "I mean, if he's really that old, how much damage could he do?"

"Why don't we look him up in Brother Dave's book?" suggested Wiglaf.

After supper, that is exactly what they did.

"Brother Dave?" called Wiglaf as he climbed up the last of the 427 steps to the library tower. "Are you here?"

"Cometh thee in!" called Brother Dave. The little monk sat behind the circulation desk, knitting a long red scarf. A candle beside him was burning low. When he saw students entering his library, his eyes lit up with joy.

Angus was the last one through the library door. Huffing and puffing, he flung himself down onto a large dragon-shaped pillow under the window.

"What canst I doeth for thee, lads and lasses?" asked Brother Dave. "I haveth some fine new books. *Jousting to Victory,* by Ray Team; *Knocking at the Castle Door,* by Lee Tussin; *Favorite Medieval Manuscripts,* by Red M. All; *All About Mead,* by Phillip Mycup; and *When Did It Happen?,* by Oliver Sudden."

"We want to find out about the dragon Grizzlegore, Bro Dave," said Janice.

"Ah, letteth me getteth thou the *Encyclopedia of Dragons,*" said Brother Dave. He hopped up and went to the stacks. He returned quickly, carrying a big, heavy book. It had a brown leather cover and a large silver clasp. He set it down on the library table and they all gathered around.

Wiglaf flipped the pages past Edith, the talkative dragon who had scared Zack, the boy from the future. He flipped past Fiffner, one of the dragons who had wounded Sir Mort. And past Gorzil, the dragon that he himself had slain, quite by accident. He turned one more page.

And there was Grizzlegore.

Chapter 3

"He looks *old*," said Erica, staring at the portrait of Grizzlegore in the book. "Really old."

"This book cameth out several years ago," said Brother Dave. "So this dragon art even older now."

Wiglaf was cheered to see that Grizzlegore was a scrawny old thing. He had bags under his drooping eyes. His forked tongue lolled from the corner of his toothless mouth. A string of drool dripped down onto his bony chest.

"He does not look like he could flame DSA," he said. Then he turned the page to see what the book had to say about the World's Oldest Living Dragon.

Full name: *Gregory Grizzlegore*

Also known as: *Geezer, G Whiz, Old Flame, Senior Moment*

Children: *Lots, but can't remember most of them*

Appearance: *Scales: green*

Horn: small, green

Eyes: two, but can't see well out of either

Teeth: fell out centuries ago

Age: *World's oldest living dragon*

Most often heard saying: *It's my birthday AGAIN?*

Biggest surprise: *Flames better with each passing year*

Hobby: *Listing the knights he's offed in alphabetical order*

Favorite thing in the world: *Flaming dragon-slaying schools*

Erica frowned. "Maybe Grizzlegore could flame DSA after all."

Angus swallowed. "Maybe we should pack up and leave like Uncle Mordred."

"Wait," said Wiglaf. "Grizzlegore has a secret weakness."

They read the last line on the page:

Secret weakness: *Take the time to learn the rhyme*

"Rhyme?" said Wiglaf. "What does that mean?"

Janice turned to Brother Dave. "What rhyme, Bro?"

"I knoweth not." Brother Dave scratched his bald pate.

"The Secret Weakness is written in rhyme," said Angus. "Maybe Grizzlegore's weakness is poetry."

"We must find out," said Erica. "Then we can fight this dragon and save DSA."

Fight the dragon? Wiglaf shuddered. The words *Flames better with each passing year* jumped out at him from the page. Just then, an idea popped into his head.

"What about Sir Mort?" he asked. "He is old. Maybe he has met Grizzlegore. Maybe he will know about the rhyme."

"Sir Mort hast evening class. Hurry and thou canst catch him," Brother Dave said.

The four sped down the tower staircase. They ran through the hallway toward the room where the old knight taught Stalking a Fire-Breather. Sounds of Sir Mort's students shrieking and laughing spilled out into the hallway.

Angus yanked open the door. The students dove for their desks and pretended to be paying attention.

Sir Mort leaped up from his desk, where he had been happily snoozing. The visor of his helmet clanked down over his face.

"Never fear, Sir Mort is here!" he yelled, struggling to draw his sword. "Show me the dragon!"

"There is no dragon, sir," said Erica. "At least not yet."

"We have come to ask you a question, Sir Mort," said Wiglaf.

Sir Mort let go of his sword and pushed up his visor. "I like questions," he said. "Not too good at answers, though. Not since Knightshredder dealt me that blow to the noggin. Now there was a dragon, sir. Full of—"

Janice snapped her gum. "Here's the question, sir," she said. "The dragon Grizzlegore has a secret weakness. It may have something to do with a rhyme. Do you know anything about it?"

"Ah, yes, Grizzlegore's rhyme," Sir Mort said dreamily. "In my salad days, I could recite it from beginning to end."

"Can you say it now, sir?" asked Erica.

"Say it! Say it!" chanted Sir Mort's class, hoping to get out of any work.

Sir Mort frowned. "How does it start? There's a first verse. I remember that. Then a second. Goes on like that, verse after verse." He thought for a long time.

At last Wiglaf said, "Sir? Do you remember why this rhyme is Grizzlegore's weakness?"

"Why, indeed?" Sir Mort nodded. "Excellent question."

"What is the answer, sir?" said Erica.

"Search me." Sir Mort shrugged. "Don't have a clue."

The next morning, Wiglaf and his friends set off once more for Ye Olde Home.

"Maybe one of the aged knights will know about the rhyme," said Wiglaf as they went.

"Not a chance," said Angus. "Those geezers are in worse shape than Sir Mort."

"You never know," said Janice. "My grandpa can't remember yesterday. Yet if you ask about his school days, he's as sharp as a sword tip."

"Sir Lancelot will know the rhyme," said Erica loyally.

"*Hola!* Hello!" Donn exclaimed as he opened the door of Ye Olde Home. "Come! I shall take you to the knights. They will be so glad to see you again."

This time Donn led them to the sitting room. Wiglaf saw that today, the aged knights were working on craft projects. Some were weaving tapestries. Others were weaving cauldron-holders. Still others held paintbrushes and were making pictures from paint-by-roman-numeral kits.

"*Señor* knights!" Donn called. "Your young friends are here to visit you!"

A few aged knights waved, but most were too busy with their crafts.

The four made their way over to where Sir Lancelot, Sir Roger, and Sir Poodleduff sat. They were molding little dragons out of clay.

"I slew a dragon once with only a dagger," Sir Poodleduff was saying.

"So?" said Sir Roger. "I once slew a dragon with only my peashooter."

"I," said Sir Lancelot, "once made the dragon Flibbergill fall down dead simply by staring him in the eye."

"Braggart!" said Sir Poodleduff.

"Liar!" said Sir Roger.

"'Tis true what Sir Lancelot says," said Erica. "He wrote about Flibbergill's death-by-staring on page three hundred and fifty-eight of *A Knight Like I*."

Sir Lancelot smiled. "So I did." He patted Erica on the head. "I like this lass!"

Erica beamed.

"Please, sirs, we have a question for you," said Janice.

"Yes," said Wiglaf. "We went to the library and looked up the secret weakness of the dragon Grizzlegore."

"The book said, 'Take the time to learn the rhyme,'" said Angus.

"Do you know what that means?" asked Erica.

"Grizzlegore?" Sir Roger shook his bald head. "Do you recall that dragon, Poodleduff?"

"Nay," said Sir Poodleduff. "Perhaps you mean

Grapplegrin. Now there's a scary dragon. Claws like sickles."

"What did I tell you?" Angus murmured. "They're just like Sir Mort."

"We mean Grizzlegore," said Wiglaf.

"I know of him," said Sir Lancelot. "When my far-older half brother, Liverspot, was a lad, he had to learn a long poem about Grizzlegore."

"Hmmm," said Sir Roger. "It's coming back to me now."

"By the time I was in school," Sir Lancelot went on, "the dragon had retired. Nobody had to learn the Grizzlegore poem."

"The Grizzlegore poem!" cried Sir Poodleduff. "Why didn't you say so?"

"Of course we know it!" cried Sir Roger. "From start to finish."

"Tell us how the rhyme is a secret weakness, sirs," said Janice.

"When we were lads," said Sir Poodleduff, "Grizzlegore was the most gold-grabbing, damsel-chasing, peasant-eating, knight-whacking, school-flaming dragon in all the land. And he could smell gold a mile away."

Sir Lancelot turned to Erica. "Let me tell you about the time I slew the great Boar of Camelot."

"Please, sir," said Erica. "We need to find out about Grizzlegore."

Sir Lancelot looked miffed.

"If Grizzlegore flew to a school," Sir Roger said, "the headmaster had to give him every bit of gold or the school was toast. Unless..."

"Unless what?" said Erica.

"Unless pupils at the school knew the rhyme," said Sir Poodleduff. "The *whole* rhyme."

"And the dance steps," added Sir Roger, giggling.

"Grizzlegore is coming to our school on April Fools' Day," Wiglaf told the old knights.

Erica added, "And our headmaster is too greedy to pay him."

"So Grizzlegore will burn down our school,"

said Angus. "Unless we can stop him."

"And if we know the rhyme, we *can* stop him," said Erica. "Can you teach it to us? Please?"

"Do dragons have tails?" cried Sir Roger.

"Do knights have steeds?" cried Sir Poodleduff.

"Of course we can!" they cried together.

Chapter 4

"'ll start off," said Sir Poodleduff.

"I'll learn it as you say it," said Erica. "I'm very good at memorizing poems."

Wiglaf crossed his fingers. He hoped that these aged knights knew the poem better than Sir Mort did.

Sir Poodleduff began:

"In days of old, when knights were bold,
And damsels knew the score,
A dragon kept a hoard of gold;
His name was Grizzlegore.

Grizzlegore lived in a cave
Outside the town of Gwail,

And he was known to flame and rave.
He had a..."

Sir Poodleduff frowned. "What was it he had, Roger?"

"*He had a spiky tail!*" exclaimed Sir Roger, pounding his cane on the hard stone floor. "I'll take it from here.

> *Grizzlegore had yellow eyes,*
> *His heart was cold and small,*
> *His fangs were of tremendous size,*
> *He lived to fight and brawl."*

Sir Lancelot yawned. Then he got up and went over to the tapestry corner.

Sir Roger recited on:

> "*Ten hundred knights did feel the heat*
> *Of Grizzlegore-y flame.*
> *Ten hundred knights knocked off their feet,*

And home they never came."

The other aged knights in Ye Olde Home gathered around Sir Roger and Sir Poodleduff. Their dry old lips moved as they, too, recited the verses they had all learned as lads.

> *"Then spaketh up Sir Percy:*
> *'This dragon we must stop!*
> *Let's show this beast no mercy.*
> *Let's whack and stab and chop!'"*

Wiglaf's stomach lurched. He hoped this was not going to turn into a very bloody poem.

Sir Poodleduff took up the verse.

> *"Sir Drake, he raised his lance up high:*
> *'For Grizzlegore—a quest!*
> *Let's seek the cave wherein he dwells,*
> *And stab him in the breast!'*

Sir Mikey and Sir Galahood,
Sir Tristam and Sir West,
Sir Dinadan, Sir Gob the Good,
They all joined in the quest.

Then spaketh up Sir Galahood,
'We'll quest for Grizzlegore!
We'll find him and we'll whack him good!
That Grizz shall gore no more.'"

Sir Poodleduff stopped and smiled. "How do you like it?" he asked.

"'Tis a fine poem," said Wiglaf, glad that it had not gotten bloody after all.

"'Tis very long," said Angus doubtfully.

"Oh, yes." All the aged knights nodded. "Very long indeed."

"Start it again, please, sirs," said Erica. "We will say it after you."

Sir Roger started in:

"In days of old, when knights were bold,
And damsels knew the score..."

Two hours later, Wiglaf's head was so stuffed
with the Grizzlegore poem that he could hardly
think. But he and his friends had managed
to learn all eight verses. They repeated them
together.

"We did it!" cried Erica.

"We can save DSA!" cried Wiglaf.

"Now teach us the dance steps," said Janice,
chewing her gum eagerly.

"But you wanted to learn the poem first," said
Sir Poodleduff.

"We did learn it," said Angus.

"No, no, no." Sir Roger shook his head. "That's
just the *beginning*."

"You mean there's *more?*" cried Janice, nearly
swallowing her gum.

"Oh, my goodness, yes," said Sir Poodleduff.

"Much more!" shouted the aged knights.

"There's an epic battle coming up," added Sir Roger, pounding his cane with glee. "Knights perish in all sorts of horrible ways."

Wiglaf felt his stomach flop. "How many verses are there?" he asked.

"Six hundred and twenty-two," said Sir Poodleduff. "Or is it twenty-three?"

"That's too long to learn by April Fools' Day," said Erica. "Even for me!"

"Oh, it takes years to learn the whole poem," said Sir Roger.

"Years and years!" agreed all the aged knights.

"Then we cannot save DSA after all," said Erica sadly.

"But the aged knights can," Wiglaf said. He turned to them. "Kind sirs, will you come to DSA on April Fools' Day and recite the Grizzlegore poem?"

But Sir Roger shook his head. "I wish we could," he said. "But that wouldn't work. It must be students from the school who recite the poem."

"Grizzlegore is very clear on that point," added Sir Poodleduff. "That way he makes sure his legend lives on."

"Oh, this is hopeless," said Erica.

"It does look that way, doesn't it?" called Sir Lancelot from the tapestry corner. Wiglaf turned and saw that he was weaving a tapestry of himself.

"Wait," said Wiglaf. "We discovered Grizzlegore's secret weakness. And we found aged knights who know the whole rhyme. We cannot give up now."

He stared at bald little Sir Roger. At skinny white-haired Sir Poodleduff. At the other old knights. Why, he could easily imagine what they had looked like when they were lads. And another idea popped into Wiglaf's head. "I wonder how good Grizzlegore's eyes are," he said, half to himself.

"He was blind as a bat fifty years ago," Sir Roger answered.

"Then all we need are uniforms," Wiglaf said, growing excited. "DSA uniforms."

"What are you talking about, Wiggie?" said Erica.

"I get it!" cried Janice. "The knights can put on uniforms and disguise themselves as DSA students! Goody—I knew something wild and crazy would happen!"

"Then the knights can come to DSA and say the rhyme for Grizzlegore!" Angus added.

"That's brilliant, Wiggie." Erica grinned. She turned to the knights. "Will you come, good sirs? And save our school?"

"We aged knights would like nothing better than to help you," said Sir Poodleduff. "But alas! We are too old to travel."

"We can't walk more than ten steps without stopping to catch our breath," said Sir Roger. "We'd never make it."

"Plus, doing the Grizzlegore dance wore us out when we were lads," said Sir Poodleduff. "If we tried it now, it would finish us off."

Just then, the dinner bell rang.

"Dinnertime already?" Sir Lancelot said. He stood up from his loom. "Excuse me for running off, lads and lasses, but I like to be first in line. I like being first at everything." And he hurried away.

As the aged knights all tottered off after him, Wiglaf heard a strange thumping sound. He turned and saw Donn coming toward them. *Thump, step. Thump, step.*

"*Perdón!*" said Donn, bowing. "Pardon me. I was nearby and could not help but overhear what you said. There is *solamente uno*—only one—person in all the world who can get these poor, weak, hunched-over knights in shape in time to help you."

"Who?" said Erica. "Tell us!"

"*Yo,*" said Donn with a sly smile. "Me. *Sí!* I can do it."

Chapter 5

"In my native country of Spain," said Donn, standing straight and tall, "I was a famous personal trainer. I was known as Don Donn."

Wiglaf saw muscles rippling under Don Donn's tunic.

"I owned a chain of popular gyms called Uno! Dos! Tres!" Don Donn said.

"One! Two! Three! Right?" said Angus.

"*Sí,*" said Don Donn. "I made getting in shape as easy as Uno! Dos! Tres! I was rolling in pesos."

"And what brought you here to Ye Olde Home, sir?" asked Wiglaf.

"Ah, that is a strange story," said Don Donn.

"Tell us, Don Donn," said Wiglaf.

"We *love* stories," said Janice, chewing loudly.

"Especially strange ones."

"*Bueno*," said Don Donn. "Three years ago, I boarded a sailing ship in Spain. I sailed for England to open more gyms. Suddenly, a terrible storm hit. Rain! Lightning! Waves as big as this castle!"

"How awful!" said Erica.

"It gets worse," said Don Donn. "A huge wave picked up the ship and smashed it to bits. The only thing left was the mast."

"That's terrible!" said Janice.

"It gets worse," said Don Donn. "All the passengers and crew were hurled into the sea. Every bone in my body was broken. But I grabbed the mast and hung on. Two others did the same. For days, we floated in the ocean, circled by vicious sea monsters."

"How horrible!" cried Angus.

"It gets worse," said Don Donn. "A big sea monster bit off my left leg."

Wiglaf's stomach lurched. "Does it get worse?"

he asked. Because if it did, he did not want to hear it.

"Only a little bit," said Don Donn. "Luckily, the water was so cold, I didn't bleed much. At last we washed ashore on an island. My comrades ripped up what was left of their shirts and bandaged what was left of my leg. I survived. When my broken bones healed, I carved myself an artificial leg out of the mast of the ship."

Wiglaf was awed. Don Donn was tough!

Janice had been listening so hard, she forgot to chew.

"Is this true?" she asked.

"*Sí!*" Don Donn rolled down the top of his left boot. Under it was a sturdy wooden leg. "Made of the finest teak." He knocked on his leg for luck.

"I still don't understand how you ended up here," said Angus.

"A passing ship rescued us," said Don Donn. "And brought us here. I'd had enough of sailing the seas and decided to stay. I had my fortune sent to me. After all I had been through, I wanted to use my training talents help those who need it most—old, battle-scarred knights. So I bought this castle. I put in a state-of-the-art Uno! Dos! Tres! gym. And I opened Ye Olde Home for Aged Knights."

"'Tis a fine home, sir," said Wiglaf.

"*Sí,*" said Don Donn. "But there is *uno problemo*—one problem. The aged knights like to talk of their glory days. But they think those days are behind them. So they have no reason to shape up. Try as I might, I have not been able to lure them into the gym. Until now."

"What's different now?" asked Janice.

"The knights want so much to help you," said Don Donn. "They want to come to your school and recite the poem. They want to save your school from Grizzlegore. That would make the aged knights heroes again."

"Can you really get these old knights to do the

Grizzlegore dance?" asked Angus.

"*Sí,*" said Don Donn. "When you have carved yourself a wooden leg from the mast of a sunken ship, you can do anything."

"Excuse me, Don Donn?" said Angus. "We have to go now or we'll miss supper at DSA."

"You will come back tomorrow, *no?*" said Don Donn.

"*Sí!*" cried Janice. "We'll help you. This is going to be so *fun!*"

"*Bueno,*" said Don Donn. "April Fools' Day is..." He counted on his fingers. "Fourteen days away. Ask your headmaster if you can stay here for two weeks. None of the aged knights can climb stairs, so there are lots of empty rooms on the second floor of the castle."

The four bid Don Donn farewell and set off for DSA.

Clouds covered the half moon. It was dark on Huntsman's Path. As they went, Wiglaf heard footsteps.

"Someone is coming toward us," he whispered.

Erica unsnapped her mini-torch from her Sir Lancelot tool belt and lit it.

Wiglaf saw two figures in the distance.

"Who goes there?" called Erica.

"Who goes *there?*" one of the figures called back.

Through the murky darkness, Wiglaf saw two lasses coming toward them.

"Erica?" said one of the lasses. "Is that you?"

Erica squinted into the darkness and said, "Rosamond?"

"Eeeeee!" Rosamond squealed. She threw her arms around Erica.

"Nice to see you, too," said Erica, slipping out of the hug. "Rosamond is the princess of West Armpitsia," she told her friends. "We go way back."

"This is Val," said Rosamond, introducing the other lass. "Princess of East Armpitsia. We've just been to DSA."

"Our headmistress sent us to borrow some gold from Mordred," said Val. "Because this dragon

Grizzlegore came and took every penny at Princess Prep."

"Zounds!" cried Janice. "What did the dragon look like?"

"He had huge pointy claws," said Rosamond. "And a spiky tail."

"Flaming drool hung down from his jaws," said Val. "Disgusting!"

Wiglaf shuddered. Grizzlegore sounded scary!

"I bet Mordred didn't lend you any gold, did he?" said Angus.

"Not a single coin," said Rosamond. "What a cheapo."

"Now we have to try Dragon Stabbers Prep," said Val. "We'd best be off."

"Byeeeee!" said Rosamond.

The lasses continued north on Huntsman's Path, while Wiglaf and his friends headed south to DSA.

One thing is for sure, Wiglaf thought. *The world's oldest living dragon is no longer retired.*

Chapter 6

"Auntie Lobelia?" said Angus when he and the others found her outside the DSA dining hall. "Where is Uncle Mordred? We need to talk to him."

"Mordie has locked himself inside his office," Lobelia said. "He's busy packing up his files and his gold. So I'm in charge at the moment." She eyed Janice. "Are you chewing gum?" she asked.

Janice drew a breath and swallowed. "Not anymore," she said.

"We need to talk to you, Auntie," said Angus. "It's important."

"Let us go to my sitting room," said Lobelia.

After hearing their story, Lady Lobelia sank into her blue velvet chair. "By Saint George's helmet!" she exclaimed. "Do you mean to tell me that only the aged knights can save DSA from Grizzlegore?"

"Yes, Auntie," said Angus. "And they'll need DSA uniforms if they are to fool the dragon into thinking they are DSA students."

"We have extra uniforms, all sizes," said Lobelia. "But they are going to need more than uniforms." Her eyes lit up. "Makeup, for starters. And wigs. I'll have everything ready by April Fools' Eve."

Wiglaf and the others ran to their dorms and packed their things.

The four took off first thing the next morning. They arrived at Ye Olde Home by mid-morning.

"*Bueno!*" said Don Donn. He showed his new training assistants to their rooms on the second floor of the castle. Janice and Erica shared a room with a view of Keep Away Mountain. Wiglaf and Angus shared a room with a view of Toenail.

Next, Don Donn took them to the gym. A

sign above the door said: UNO! DOS! TRES!

Janice whistled as they entered. "This is one fine gym," she said. "It's even better than the one we had at Dragon Whackers."

Wiglaf had never seen a gym. DSA did not have one, as Mordred believed that his students got plenty of exercise scrubbing the school. Now Wiglaf gawked at all the odd-looking machines and equipment. Ropes hung from the ceiling. An iron chinning bar had been bolted high in a doorway. There were many different sizes of balls and weights. Mats had been spread out on the floor. And in one corner sat a shiny rowboat with oars.

Don Donn spent the morning showing the four how to do proper Uno! Dos! Tres! chin-ups, sit-ups, push-ups, and jumping jacks. He showed them how to work all the machines. Then he said, "Here are Uno! Dos! Tres! ribbons to wear." He handed them out. "That will show that you are my official assistant trainers."

How proud Wiglaf was as he pinned his ribbon onto his tunic.

"The aged knights will be having their lunch now," said Don Donn. "Why do we not join them?"

They walked down the hallway and into the dining hall.

"Who ate my sticky bun?" cried one aged knight.

"There's no meat in my meat pie!" cried another.

All the complaining reminded Wiglaf of lunchtime at DSA.

"Ah, the students," said Sir Poodleduff, beckoning them over to his table.

The four sat down.

"They've come back to hear more of the poem, Roger," said Sir Poodleduff. "Where were we?"

"I know," said Sir Roger. And he began reciting.

"The dragon rose inside his cave.
He lowered his massive head.
The knights were bold and very brave,
Yet from the cave they fled.

Sir Percy spake: 'We need a plan!'
Sir Gob the Good spake, 'Right.'
And so the knights all, to a man,
Made plans all through the night."

"Perdón!" said Don Donn. "Pardon me for interrupting, Sir Roger. But you knights wish to be the heroes who save DSA from Grizzlegore, no?"

"We wish we could!" all the knights cried.

All except Sir Lancelot, who kept eating his sticky bun.

"Bueno!" said Don Donn. "Then I have good news for you. You *can* go to DSA. You can be heroes again."

Erica stood up. "Good sirs, Don Donn and his new assistants—us!—are going to get you back into knightly shape," she announced. "We will work with you for the next two weeks using his famous Uno! Dos! Tres! training method."

Angus stood now. "At the end of two weeks, you will be strong enough to travel to DSA."

Janice popped up next. "Strong enough to recite the whole Grizzlegore poem."

Now Wiglaf stood with the others. "Strong enough to do the Grizzlegore dance. And save our school from the dragon."

"Hooray for us!" cried Sir Poodleduff.

And all the aged knights began clapping and stomping.

"Hah!" cried Sir Lancelot as the cheering died down. "Double hah!"

The room grew very still.

"Oh, come on," Sir Lancelot said to the aged knights. "You don't really think a few days in a gym is going to make any difference, do you? It will just make you tired. And sore. It will make you cranky. But it will not turn you into heroes again. No way."

"Wanna bet, Lance?" cried Sir Roger.

"Watch us!" cried Sir Poodleduff.

Now Don Donn rose to stand. "Listen to me, senior *señores*," he said. "Uno! Dos!

Tres! works. I swear it on my wooden leg. Any knights who wish to train, please stand...or if you have trouble standing, please raise your right hand."

Many a right hand went up in the dining hall.

"*Bueno*, senior *señores*," said Don Donn. "Then let's get started." He turned to Sir Lancelot.

"Don't look at me," Sir Lancelot said. "I'm happy as I am. Doing nothing."

Chapter 7

"Welcome to day one of Knightly Training Camp," said Don Donn as sixteen aged knights tottered and shuffled into the gym.

"Gadzooks!" exclaimed Sir Poodleduff, looking around. "What's all this stuff for?"

"My able training assistants will show you how to do everything," Don Donn promised. "Now, line up."

The knights were split into groups of four. Sir Poodleduff, Sir Knickerknot, and two others came shuffling over to Wiglaf.

As Wiglaf helped his knights totter over to the chinning bar, he saw Sir Lancelot leaning in the gym doorway.

"Watch how I grab hold and pull up until my

chin touches the bar," Wiglaf said. He was not very strong. But with the aged knights watching him, he managed to do three passable chin-ups. He dropped to the floor. "Your turn, Sir Poodleduff."

Don Donn came by. He and Wiglaf gave Sir Poodleduff a boost. The aged knight took hold of the bar.

"You can do it!" Wiglaf said.

"Fat chance!" called Sir Lancelot.

"Pull yourself up!" said Don Donn.

"I am pulling!" cried Sir Poodleduff. Then he let go.

"See?" crowed Sir Lancelot. "What did I tell you?"

Sir Knickerknot and the other aged knights took their turns. Not one of them could do a chin-up. Nor could they lift the oars on the rowing machine. Leaping over the pommel horse was out of the question.

When the dinner bell clanged, the DSA students sat at a table with Don Donn. Once

Lancelot left, they were the only ones in the dining hall. All the aged knights were so pooped, they had gone straight to bed.

"It's hopeless," Janice said. "My group can hardly breathe."

"Sir Roger can't do anything," said Angus. "And if I help him, he tries to beat me with his cane."

"Sir Dribblechin can bend down and touch his knees," said Erica. "The rest of my crew can't even do that!"

"Sir Knickerknot only looked at the equipment and he fell asleep," reported Wiglaf.

"Bueno!" said Don Donn. "Good."

"Not so *bueno*, sir," said Erica. "They are all miserable failures."

"No one ever succeeds without failing at the start," said Don Donn. "Tomorrow you will see a difference."

The next day Wiglaf saw that the aged knights did do a teeny-weeny bit better. Sir Poodleduff managed to hold the chinning bar with both hands. And, with great effort, he bent his elbows.

"Hooray!" cheered Wiglaf. "You made progress."

Sir Knickerknot managed to climb into the rowing machine and pick up the oars before falling asleep.

After an hour of training, Don Donn said, "Knights, take a seat on a mat."

It took some time for the knights to get their old bodies into sitting positions.

"Close your eyes, senior *señores*," said Don Donn. "Imagine—it is April Fools' Day. Picture yourselves in bright blue tunics, riding your steeds toward DSA. You are trim and fit, just as you were in your glory days."

Wiglaf saw that the old knights were smiling.

"Now, picture yourselves facing the dragon," said Don Donn. "You stare him in the eye and begin saying the poem."

Some of the aged knights began silently mouthing the words.

"Now," said Don Donn, "imagine breaking into the Grizzlegore dance."

"Whoa!" cried Sir Poodleduff. He kept his eyes closed, but he started moving his hands and feet.

"Yessss," cried Sir Roger, doing the same.

"Feast your eyes on us, you greedy dragon!" cried Sir Knickerknot.

"Well done," Don Donn said at last. "Open your eyes. An excellent beginning. Report to the gym tomorrow morning at seven bells."

The old knights struggled to their feet. They limped out of the gym.

But Sir Poodleduff stayed behind. He walked over to the chinning bar, and grabbed hold. He pulled. He gritted his teeth. His face turned red. And he did one chin-up.

"Hooray, Sir Poodleduff!" cried Wiglaf. "Outstanding!"

He turned to Don Donn. "This works!" he said.

"*Sí,*" said Don Donn. "It always does."

Knightly Training Camp went on for days. The

aged knights worked hard. Every day, they got a little bit stronger. They never complained about the exercises. Only about the new health food Don Donn served them.

Some days, Sir Lancelot would slouch in the doorway of the gym.

"*Señor* Lancelot!" called Don Donn. "Come show these aged knights how to do a chin-up!"

Sir Lancelot only shook his head. "Why should I?" he said. "I'm not training to go off on any silly quest."

As training went on, the aged knights saw real progress.

On day five, Sir Poodleduff did three chin-ups.

On day seven, Sir Roger tossed aside his cane. "Good riddance!" he cried.

On day eight, Sir Knickerknot climbed all the way up the rope and slapped the ceiling. "Yessss!" he cried.

On day nine, Sir Roger walked to the chinning bar.

"Sir Roger! Sir Roger! He's our man!" cheered Angus. "He can do chin-ups, yes, he can!"

Sir Roger jumped up, grabbed the bar, and did twelve chin-ups.

"Yay!" the aged knights cheered as he let go of the bar. "Hooray!"

Every day, Don Donn had the knights close their eyes and imagine themselves having glory days once more.

By day ten, Sir Poodleduff was standing straight and tall. He looked twenty years younger than he had when Wiglaf had first seen him. And Sir Roger had muscles in his arms and a fire in his eyes.

At the end of day eleven, the aged knights went over to Don Donn and his assistant trainers.

"We are living proof that Uno! Dos! Tres! works, Don Donn," said Sir Poodleduff. He turned around to show off his fine posture.

"*Sí!*" said Don Donn.

"But starting tomorrow morning," put in Sir Roger, "we need some time off."

Don Donn frowned. "But why?"

"If we are going to save DSA from Grizzlegore," Sir Roger said, "we need time to practice our dance."

Don Donn broke into a grin. *"Bueno!"* he said. "We can work that into the training routine. *No problemo!"*

"Hey, Roger," said Janice. "Can you teach us the dance?"

"Do dragons have scales?" said Sir Roger.

"Do knights have armor?" said Sir Poodleduff.

"Of course we can!" cried all the aged knights together.

"All right!" yelled Janice. She blew a bubble bigger and bigger until it popped. "Tomorrow we rock!"

The next morning, Wiglaf and the others rushed to the gym.

The aged knights were already there.

"Come on over!" called Sir Poodleduff when

he saw them. "We've been practicing since dawn."

"Ready, Poodleduff?" said Sir Roger. "Let's demo."

The two old knights stood side by side. With a jump, they turned to face each other and drew imaginary swords. They called out:

"In days of old, when knights were bold..."

They put their index fingers to their foreheads and said:

"And damsels knew the score..."

Sir Poodleduff and Sir Roger spread out their fingers at the sides of their heads and made terrible angry faces:

"A dragon kept a hoard of gold..."

Now they each held up their right hand in the shape of a claw.

"His name was Grizzlegore."

"We can do that!" cried Erica. "Watch!"

The four DSA students did the Grizzlegore moves.

"Muy bueno!" said Don Donn, who had come

into the gym unnoticed. "Very good!"

The aged knights said the next verse of the poem and demonstrated the dance steps:

> "Grizzlegore lived in a cave
> Outside the town of Gwail,
> And he was known to flame and rave.
> He had a spiky tail."

Every time they said Grizzlegore's name, they made the sign of the claw with their aged hands. But when they got to the part where Grizzlegore "flamed and raved," the old knights went wild. They spun around, jumped up, and fell to the floor in splits.

"Good sirs!" cried Wiglaf. "Are you all right?"

"Yes, yes," said Sir Poodleduff, pushing himself up to his hands and knees. "It's all part of the dance."

Sir Roger said, "Actually, I seem to be stuck here."

After that, the aged knights decided to explain

the wilder dance moves to Wiglaf and his friends, and not go all out until they met Grizzlegore.

Janice was a natural at the Grizzlegore dance—especially the wild and crazy parts. Erica was great at the hand motions. Angus's best moves were shakes and shimmies. Wiglaf discovered he had a talent for the quick spin and the splits. He thought he had never worked so hard in his life. By the time they got to verse seven, he and his friends were panting for breath and soaked with sweat.

That evening the four DSA students were the first in bed.

Day thirteen arrived. The aged knights and the DSA students spent the morning polishing their dance steps.

"Muy, muy bueno!" cried Don Donn, watching them dance through the first twenty-five verses. "You look like pros."

After lunch, the knights went back to their usual Uno! Dos! Tres! routine. As they went through their final workout, Sir Lancelot appeared at the gym door. He had a smirk on his face.

"*Hola, Señor* Lancelot," Don Donn said. "They are ready. You can join in. You have watched every day. You must know all the moves."

"You can do it, sir!" cried Erica.

"You can!" cried Wiglaf.

"I know I *can*," said Sir Lancelot. "It's just, do I *want* to? And the answer is 'I don't.' "

He turned and stalked off.

Wiglaf thought Erica looked like she might cry.

Chapter 8

April Fools' Day dawned clear and sunny. The aged knights and training assistants ate a hearty breakfast. Then they went outside.

"Bring out our noble steeds!" cried Sir Poodleduff.

"Sorry," said Don Donn as he drove a large hay wagon pulled by two gray horses out of the stable. "No steeds."

"No problemo," said Sir Roger. He and the other aged knights jumped onto the back of the wagon. Wiglaf and his friends jumped on, too.

"Giddyap, Rosa! Giddyap, Bella!" Don Donn said to his horses. "Let's go!"

The ride was bumpy, but none of the aged knights complained. Wiglaf thought they all seemed glad to be out in the world again.

At last, a dark stone castle came into view.

"There it is!" Erica said, pointing. "Dragon Slayers' Academy."

Wiglaf looked with fondness at his school. How he hoped the aged knights would be able to save it from Grizzlegore's flames.

Don Donn stopped the hay wagon at the foot of the drawbridge. All his passengers hopped off.

"Uncle Mordred!" called Angus as he ran across the drawbridge. "Auntie Lobelia!" He pounded on the great wooden doors.

Wiglaf waited on the bridge with Erica, Janice, Don Donn, and the aged knights. He stared up at the castle. The great wooden doors were shut. The iron bars had been let down in front of the doors. All the windows were shuttered. DSA was ready for Grizzlegore.

Angus pounded on the doors again. "Open up!" he cried. "We know how to save DSA from Grizzlegore!"

At last Frypot, the school cook, flung open the doors. He stared past Angus at the ragged group of aged knights.

"Looking for a bite to eat, are you, my good fellows?" he asked. "Come in. I'll fix you some of my good lumpen pudding."

"Lumpen pudding?" cried one of the aged knights. "That's what they served at school when we were lads!"

"We didn't like it then," said another knight. "And we don't like it now."

Before Frypot had a chance to offer them any of his eel stew, Lobelia came up behind him.

"Welcome, knights!" she said. "Thank you for coming."

"*Señorita* L.," Don Donn said, bowing. He took Lady Lobelia's hand and brought it to his lips. "What a pleasure to see you once more."

"Oh, Donn!" squealed Lady Lobelia. "Likewise!"

Angus rolled his eyes. "Auntie," he groaned.

"Please, everyone, come in!" said Lobelia.

They all walked through the gatehouse and into the castle yard.

Wiglaf was surprised to see Mordred in the castle yard. He had on his red silk traveling cloak and hat. He was sitting by the scrubbing block on a huge pile of luggage.

"The students are in class," Lobelia said, keeping her voice low. "I am trying to keep things as they always are. I don't want anyone to panic because a dragon is coming." She glanced at Mordred and rolled her eyes. "Come to my sitting room, knights. You, too, Donn." She smiled and batted her eyes. "Angus?" she added. "You and your friends come help me get these knights into their DSA uniforms."

"This looks just like my old school," said Sir Poodleduff as they headed for the castle.

"Makes me feel like a lad again," said Sir Roger.

When they entered Lady Lobelia's sitting room, Wiglaf saw that she had laid out many

DSA uniforms by size.

"Pick out your size," said Lobelia. "You can go behind that screen to change."

Sir Poodleduff and nine other aged knights quickly grabbed up the ten lads' uniforms. They scurried behind the screen.

"All that's left are lasses' uniforms!" cried Sir Roger.

"The point is to fool Grizzlegore," said Lady Lobelia. "Go on, pick out a uniform."

Sir Roger and the other knights did not look happy as they picked up their lasses' uniforms. They, too, went behind the screen.

Minutes later, all the knights came out again, clad in DSA tunics and breeches.

Wiglaf's eyes grew wide as he looked at the many spindly old legs sticking out from under the uniforms. And at the white-haired heads above the tunics. Wiglaf swallowed. *Would Grizzlegore be fooled?* He hoped so.

"I feel like a lad again!" exclaimed Sir Poodleduff.

He turned around to show off his uniform.

"Well, I don't," said Sir Roger, who was clad in one of the lasses' uniforms. He folded his arms across his chest.

"Maybe this will help," said Lobelia. She plopped a wig of blond curls onto his bald pate. Then she stepped back to admire it. "Very nice!" she said.

She began putting wigs of different colors on all the aged knights dressed as lasses.

Wiglaf hurried over to Sir Roger. "You are indeed a hero, sir," Wiglaf told him. "No matter how you are dressed."

"Thank you, lad," said Sir Roger, perking up. "I needed that."

"We need a dress rehearsal of the dance moves with the students," said Sir Poodleduff. "Let us go out to the castle yard."

Wiglaf and his friends went out to the yard ahead of Don Donn and the aged knights. They saw Mordred still sitting on his bags.

"Sir!" called Wiglaf as he, Erica, and Janice hurried over to Mordred. "We have brought sixteen knights from Ye Olde—"

"Enough!" boomed Mordred, holding up a gold-ringed hand. "Did you catch sight of my scout Yorick on your way here?"

"No, sir," said Erica.

Mordred frowned. "He was supposed to be here an hour ago to drive me and my gold to—" He looked at them suspiciously. "—to a safe place."

"There is no need to hide your gold from Grizzlegore now, sir," said Janice.

"No?" Mordred raised one bushy eyebrow.

"No, Uncle," said Angus. "The aged knights will save us from the dragon."

Mordred frowned. "Those old bags of bones don't stand a chance against Grizzlegore."

"They know his secret weakness, sir," said Wiglaf. "'Tis a poem. And they shall recite it to him."

"You mean...my gold may be saved?" asked

Mordred eagerly.

"Yes, Uncle," said Angus. "Your gold *will* be saved."

Mordred grinned. "Well, what are you lads and lasses waiting for?" he cried. "Pick up my luggage! Take it to my office. Get a move on, now. Chop-chop!"

Wiglaf had just picked up a heavy bag when there was a commotion at the castle doors. He turned and saw DSA students pouring forth into the castle yard.

"Egad!" cried Mordred. "Don't let those ruffians near my gold!"

"They're not ruffians, Uncle," said Angus. "They are your students."

"Let us out of there!" the students cried, running for the gatehouse.

Erica ran in front of them. "As the Future Dragon Slayer of the Month, I order you to stop!" she cried.

All the lads and lasses stopped.

"There is no need to flee," said Erica.

"But a dragon is coming to flame the school!" cried Charley Marley.

"A dragon is coming," said Erica. "But he won't flame the school. Because we have a secret weapon!"

"All right!" cheered the lads and lasses. "A secret weapon!"

"What is the secret weapon?" asked Farley Marley.

Just then the castle doors opened again. The aged knights came down the steps, dressed in DSA uniforms.

"Behold!" said Erica, pointing to the castle doors. "Our secret weapon!"

All the lads and lasses turned toward the doors. When they saw the aged knights in the DSA uniforms, their jaws dropped open.

"*That's* your secret weapon?" cried Barley Marley.

"A bunch of geezers?" cried Charley Marley.

Without waiting for an answer, they ran screaming for the gatehouse.

"Stop!" Erica called after them. "Wait!"

But they ran on. And as they ran, the sky above darkened.

Wiglaf looked up. Great black clouds were rolling across the sky.

The students stopped and looked up, too. The castle yard grew still.

A sudden whoosh of bright orange flame cut through the clouds. And a voice rang out above them:

"THE WORLD'S OLDEST LIVING DRAGON—GRIZZLEGORE—IS HERE! COME OUT TO GREET ME!"

Chapter 9

t the sound of Grizzlegore's voice, Mordred began to scream.

All the students at the gatehouse screamed, too.

"Cancel the dress rehearsal," Sir Poodleduff called calmly over their screams. "Students, line up. Knights, get behind them."

Wiglaf, Angus, and Janice lined up as Sir Poodleduff had asked.

But Erica ran to the gatehouse.

"As Future Dragon Slayer of the Month, I order you to stop screaming!" she yelled.

They stopped.

"You have to help save DSA," she told them. "Go over with the aged knights. Crowd around them. That will make it look like they are students."

"Yes, Erica," said Charley Marley.

"Keep your eyes on Wiglaf, Janice, Angus, and me," she told them. "Follow what we do. For if we fail, DSA will go up in flames!"

"Yes, Erica!" they all said.

Erica ran back to the front of the formation. The other students crowded in among the aged knights.

"Forward, march!" cried Sir Poodleduff.

And all together, they marched through the gatehouse, over the drawbridge, and onto the grass in front of DSA.

Emboldened by such a large crowd, Mordred scampered after them.

Wiglaf's heart beat like a drum as he went. Verses of the Grizzlegore poem skipped around inside his brain. Bits of the dance steps popped into his head. He felt dizzy.

"Look! Look!" everyone started shouting.

Wiglaf looked up. At first, he did not see Grizzlegore. Then he spotted the dragon curled on a tree branch not far from the drawbridge. He was a sickly green color. The horn on his nose flopped sadly over to one side. He was badly bent and had a hump on his back.

"My, my," said Grizzlegore, his voice trembling with age. "How nice that the whole school is coming out to greet me."

The creature smiled. Wiglaf thought that for the world's oldest living dragon, he sure had a nice new set of false fangs.

"Let's not waste time," said Grizzlegore. "I'm already old as the hills. Who knows how much time I have left? So! Hand over your gold and I'll be gone."

Mordred elbowed his way to the front of the group.

"We will give you no gold, dragon!" he cried.

The shocked dragon's mouth dropped wide open.

Wiglaf watched, horrified, as his fangs fell from his mouth.

"Drat my dentist!" cried the dragon. "There goes another set of choppers!"

Then from his toothless mouth he shot an angry tongue of flame. Flame so hot that everyone began to cough and sputter. Mordred's hair began to smoke.

"Zounds!" cried Mordred. "I am on fire!"

He zoomed over to the moat and plunged his head into the water.

"Go get the gold," Grizzlegore growled as best he could without his fangs. "Bring it to me. Now! Or your school is toast."

"Ready, and!" called Sir Poodleduff.

And everyone who had taken the time to learn the rhyme shouted out:

"In days of old, when knights were bold..."

Wiglaf and Erica jumped to face each other. They drew imaginary swords.

Behind them, the aged knights and DSA students followed along.

"And damsels knew the score..."

Everyone put their index fingers to their foreheads.

"A dragon kept a hoard of gold..."

Now they put their fingers up to their heads and made terrible, angry faces.

"His name was Grizzlegore."

Everyone held up their right hands in the shape of a claw.

"By my scales!" cried the delighted dragon. "You know the poem! Well, go on. Go on!"

And so they did. Those who knew the rhyme recited it. And everyone did their best with the dance.

> *"Grizzlegore lived in a cave*
> *Outside the town of Gwail,*
> *And he was known to flame and rave.*
> *He had a spiky tail."*

After they said the first eight verses, the aged knights had to recite on their own. But by that

time, Grizzlegore was writhing with happiness at hearing himself immortalized in his poem. No one had anything to fear from this fire-breather.

The aged knights kept reciting.

"The dragon rose inside his cave.
He lowered his massive head.
The knights were bold and very brave,
Yet from the cave they fled."

Now Grizzlegore held up a claw for them to stop.

"That is one of my favorite verses," he told them. "When the knights flee from the cave? I just love that."

Mordred dared to speak again. "Dragon," he said, "there will be no more talk of wanting my gold, will there?"

Grizzlegore shook his old head. "No, saying the rhyme is payment enough," he said. "Although it does leave me a bit short of cash."

Before he thought about it, Wiglaf spoke up. "You have the gold from the other dragon schools," he said. "Isn't that enough?"

"Enough?" huffed Grizzlegore, puffing smoke from his nose. "You think I have enough?"

Wiglaf trembled as he nodded.

"Then you know nothing of what surgeons are charging these days," the dragon said. "Why, those greedy sawbones won't fix a simple ingrown claw for under six thousand ducats."

"That's what you want the gold for?" cried Sir Roger. "An operation?"

Grizzlegore nodded. "When you've lived as long as I have, things get broken," he said. "The old ticker is still going strong. I have a few centuries ahead of me yet. But I can hardly see the horn at the end of my snout anymore. My bones haven't held up. Both my hips are shot. My knees wobble like jelly custard. My ankles are as weak as newborn kittens. And oh, my aching back!"

"We feel your pain," said Sir Poodleduff.

The dragon stared at him. Everyone was very still.

Grizzlegore glared at Sir Poodleduff. "You don't know what it's like to be old!"

"No, of course we don't," said Sir Poodleduff quickly. "I only meant that we lads and lasses *will* feel your pain one day, when we are old—like you."

Grizzlegore nodded, seeming to accept this explanation. "My wings are the only things still working," he went on. "But who knows how long they'll last?"

Now Don Donn stepped forward. He bowed before the dragon.

"*Hola, Señor* Grizzlegore," he said. "Perhaps I can help you. *Por favor*—please, may I take a look at your ankles? I am a trainer. Perhaps I can show you a few exercises to get them back in shape."

"What have I got to lose?" said Grizzlegore. He slithered down from the tree and eased himself into a sitting position. He held out his left back paw.

"*Uno,*" said Don Donn. Taking the dragon's

paw in his hands, he circled it sundial-wise a few times, then counter-sundial-wise. He had the dragon try it.

"*Dos*," said Don Donn. He had the dragon push his paw against his hand.

"*Tres*," said Don Donn. "Close your eyes and picture yourself running like a young dragon again."

Grizzlegore did as Don Donn said. A smile appeared on his ancient face.

"*Bueno!*" said Don Donn. "Let me see you put some weight on this paw."

Grizzlegore pushed himself up to a stand. He took a step on the left paw. "Astonishing!" he cried. "Why, it feels fine."

He sat down again quickly, and held out his right rear paw. As Don Donn began to circle it, Grizzlegore said, "Maybe I don't need an operation after all. Maybe I need exercise."

"*Sí*," agreed Don Donn. "We will work on your knees next."

While Don Donn took Grizzlegore through

his exercises, Mordred, Lobelia, the aged knights, and all the students went back into the DSA castle. The students took the shutters off the slits in the castle walls. After that, Frypot served an extra-lumpy lumpen pudding for lunch. Then everyone went outside to check on Don Donn and Grizzlegore.

Wiglaf gasped when he saw the dragon. Grizzlegore's horn sat upright on his nose. He was walking tall and proud.

"Zounds!" cried Mordred. "Is there magic afoot?"

"Wouldn't know I was the world's oldest living dragon now, would you?" asked Grizzlegore, turning around so they could see him from all sides.

"No!" everyone cried.

Don Donn stood beside Grizzlegore, smiling proudly.

"Oh, Donn!" cried Lady Lobelia, beaming. "You are my hero!"

"*Gracias, Señorita*," said Don Donn, kissing her hand again.

"Ugh," said Angus. "This looks bad."

Now the dragon turned to Don Donn. "*Muchas gracias*, Don Donn," he said.

"You speak Spanish?" said Don Donn, surprised.

"*Sí*," said Grizzlegore. "When you've lived as long as I have, you speak everything." He smiled. "All my gold is yours, Don Donn. Take it."

"*Gracias*," said Don Donn. "Thank you. But it is not really your gold, is it?"

"It is now," said Grizzlegore. "And I give it all to you."

"*Por favor*," said Don Donn. "Please. Give it back to the schools."

Grizzlegore rolled his eyes. "All right. I shall. But how can I repay you, Don Donn?"

"I'll help you think of something, Donn," said Lobelia.

Before Don Donn could answer, a horse and rider appeared in the distance. Someone was riding toward DSA.

"Who could that be?" asked Wiglaf.

Erica squinted into the distance. "It is...Sir

Lancelot!" she cried.

The once-perfect knight rode up to where everyone was gathered outside of DSA. His steed sagged badly under his weight. Yet something about Sir Lancelot looked different now. For one thing, he had managed to squeeze into his armor.

"Oh, sir!" cried Erica. "How good to see you mounted upon your steed once more!"

"Thank you, lass," he said.

"I wonder how glad his steed is of it," murmured Janice.

"You are in your armor, sir," said Wiglaf. "Have you taken up the knightly life again?"

"I have," said Sir Lancelot. "And I watched enough of the Uno! Dos! Tres! method to know what to do. Soon I will look like the perfect knight again."

"What made you change your mind, sir?" asked Janice.

"It was the aged knights," said Sir Lancelot.

"Shhh!" said Erica. "The dragon thinks they're

kids like us."

"They showed me that *being* the best is not as important as *trying* your best," said Sir Lancelot.

"Now *that* sounds like Sir Lancelot!" cried Erica.

"I shall try my best to be a good knight," said Sir Lancelot. "And I shall try my best to run Leon out of business and get my catalog going again."

"Oh, sir!" cried Erica, tears of joy springing to her eyes. "Thank you!"

Sir Lancelot nodded. Then he picked up his reins and his steed hobbled off toward new adventures in the Dark Forest.

"Good-bye, sir!" cried Erica. "Good-bye!"

When Sir Lancelot was out of sight, Don Donn turned to the dragon.

"*Señor* Grizzlegore," he said. "I have thought of a way you can repay me."

"Anything," said Grizzlegore.

"Come back with me to Ye Olde Home for Aged Knights," said Don Donn. "You can have the whole second floor of the castle."

"Three meals a day?" said Grizzlegore.

Don Donn nodded.

"Fresh linens on the bed every week?" said Grizzlegore.

"*Sí*," said Don Donn. "I will help you with your exercises. And in return, perhaps now and then you could spar with my aged knights. Let them feel the weight of the lance in their hands once more. Let them relive their glory days."

"Just for show, right?" said Grizzlegore. "No wounds."

"No wounds," said Don Donn.

"And on cold winter evenings," put in Sir Poodleduff, "we can recite—I mean *they* can recite—your poem."

"Complete with dance steps!" added Sir Roger.

"It's a deal!" cried Grizzlegore.

Now Grizzlegore turned to Mordred. "I shall never forget how good fortune smiled upon me here at Dragon Slayers' Academy," he said.

Mordred's violet eyes shone. "Yes, dear dragon, and were you thinking, perhaps... of some reward? A small gift to the school? Or a large one! We could name a new addition after you. The Grizzlegore Wing. How do you like the sound of that?"

Grizzlegore smiled a fangless smile. "Perhaps I could leave DSA a little something in my will," he said.

"I was hoping for sooner," said Mordred. "But you are very old. So who knows? Thank you, dragon."

Then Grizzlegore hopped onto the wagon. "I'm a little too tuckered out to fly," he said.

Before Don Donn climbed up into the driver's seat, he whispered to Wiglaf, "Tell the old lads to change back into their clothes. I will return for them, and Grizzlegore will never be any the wiser."

"Farewell, my dear Donn!" called Lady Lobelia, waving a sky blue hankie.

"*Adiós, Señorita* Lobelia," said Don Donn. He blew her a kiss. "I'll be back to see you soon!"

Then Don Donn and the dragon drove off up

Huntsman's Path.

"Come back and visit!" Don Donn and Grizzlegore called back to the students.

"We will!" cried Janice.

"Farewell, Grizzlegore!" Wiglaf and the others called after them.

Everyone waved until the wagon had vanished from sight. Then everyone headed for the DSA castle.

"We did it, Wiggie," Erica said as they went.

"Thanks to the geezers." Janice wrapped her arm around Sir Poodleduff.

Wiglaf looked up at DSA. It was filled with cobwebs and creeping, crawling bugs. The teachers were oddballs. And it was a daily challenge to swallow the food that Frypot cooked. Still, Wiglaf was very happy to be walking into the cold, dark, crumbling castle that was his school.

"We did," Wiglaf replied to his friends and to the old knights. "We all saved DSA from the dragon."

Rhyme of the Ancient Dragon
Verses I–XXIV

In days of old, when knights were bold,
And damsels knew the score,
A dragon kept a hoard of gold;
His name was Grizzlegore.

Grizzlegore lived in a cave
Outside the town of Gwail,
And he was known to flame and rave.
He had a spiky tail.

Grizzlegore had yellow eyes,
His heart was cold and small,
His fangs were of tremendous size,
He lived to fight and brawl.

Ten hundred knights did feel the heat
Of Grizzlegore-y flame.
Ten hundred knights knocked off their feet,
And home they never came.

Then spaketh up Sir Percy:
"This dragon we must stop!
Let's show this beast no mercy.
Let's whack and stab and chop!"

Sir Drake, he raised his lance up high:
"For Grizzlegore—a quest!
Let's seek the cave wherein he dwells,
And stab him in the breast!"

Sir Mikey and Sir Galahood
Sir Tristam and Sir West,
Sir Dinadan, Sir Gob the Good,
They all joined in the quest.

Then spaketh up Sir Galahood,
"We'll quest for Grizzlegore!
We'll find him and we'll whack him good!
That Grizz shall gore no more."

The dragon rose inside his cave.
He lowered his massive head.
The knights were bold and very brave,
Yet from the cave they fled.

Sir Percy spake: "We need a plan!"
Sir Gob the Good spake, "Right."
And so the knights all, to a man,
Made plans all through the night.

And when the sun rose in the sky,
They had a plan so brave.
They lifted lance and sword on high,
And set off for the cave.

Outside the cave they lay in wait,
Their lances firm in hand.
The dragon slept till after eight,
The knights, they kept their stand.

They waited and they waited, but
No dragon did appear.
At last spake up Sir Gob: "Tut, tut!
There's something wrong, I fear."

And so the knights crept two by two,
Into the dragon's lair.
They shone their torches—wouldn't you?
But found the cave quite bare.

"Alas! Alas!" cried Galahood.
"Alack-a-day!" cried West.
"Oh, piffle!" cried Sir Gob the Good,
"We've failed in our quest!"

And there and then, from deep inside
The cave, a voice did shout:
"You knights had better run and hide,
Before I sniff you out!"

They turned as one to flee that cave,
But in its mouth they stuck.
Sir Percy spake: "We must be brave,
For we are out of luck."

They felt the dragon's steamy breath
Upon their armored backs.
Sir Gob, he spake: "Prepare for death!
And say your last 'alacks'!"

Then small Sir Mikey wiggled free,
He turned to Grizzlegore.
He spake: "Vile dragon, hear our plea!
Or we shall be no more."

The dragon turned his yellow eyes
Upon the helpless men.
"All right, I'll close my eyes, you guys,
And count from one to ten."

Sir Percy and Sir Galahood,
Sirs West and Tristam, too,
Sir Dinadan, Sir Gob the Good,
They spake: "Oh, Grizzlegore, thank you!"

The dragon shut his yellow eyes.
The knights, they wriggled free.
"One! Two! Three!" the dragon cried.
The knights, how they did flee.

Sir Mikey spake: "So kind and bold
This dragon was this day.
Perhaps his heart is not so cold.
He let us get away!"

From deep inside his Gwaily cave,
The dragon smiled and flamed.
"Oh, come back soon, you armored knaves,
So we can play our games."

Dragon Slayers' Academy™ 17

HAIL! HAIL!
CAMP DRAGONONKA!

It's summer vacation, and DSA is closed.
What's a kid to do? Go to summer camp,
of course! Wiglaf and friends head to Camp
Dragononka, where there's one surprise after
another. But then Dudwin, Wiglaf's brother, starts
to talk about a dragon ghost, and strange things
begin to happen . . . Someone (or some*thing*)
wants them to leave!

**There's twice as much DSA fun in this
twice-as-long Super Special!**

FRIGHT NIGHT!

Adapted by Kate Howard

SCHOLASTIC INC.

LEGO, the LEGO logo, the Brick and Knob configurations, the Minifigure, and NEXO KNIGHTS are trademarks of the LEGO Group. All rights reserved. © 2016 The LEGO Group. Produced by Scholastic Inc. under license from The LEGO Group.

Published by Scholastic Inc., *Publishers since 1920.* SCHOLASTIC and associated logos are trademarks and/or registered trademarks of Scholastic Inc.

ISBN 978-0-545-92555-6

10 9 8 7 6 5 4 3 2 1   16 17 18 19 20

Printed in the U.S.A.   40
First printing 2016
Book design by Rick DeMonico

CONTENTS

From the Files of Merlok 2.0 iv

Chapter 1 1

Chapter 2 17

Chapter 3 27

Chapter 4 42

Chapter 5 51

Chapter 6 64

Greetings, and welcome to the Files of Merlok 2.0—that's me! Now where was I . . . Ah, yes! For over one hundred years, the kingdom of Knighton knew only peace. In the capital city of Knightonia, humans and Squirebots began to live side-by-side, surrounded by the city's technical marvels—like the awe-inspiring Beam Bridges or the state-of-the-art Joustdome.

I, Merlok the wizard, used my magic to help the kingdom whenever I could. My greatest task was to keep the dangerous Books of Dark Magic locked away in my library. The most wicked of these books was The Book of Monsters. Under my very nose, this clever book plotted to escape from my library.

One day, the book found the perfect puppet for its plans: Jestro, the court jester. Jestro had no friends in the kingdom except for Clay Moorington. Clay tried to be kind to the jester, but everyone else thought Jestro was a joke—and not the funny kind. Jestro was tired of everyone laughing at him instead of with him.

Lonely and eager to prove that he was nothing to be laughed at, Jestro was a perfect target for The Book of Monsters' offer. If Jestro freed it, together they could unleash an evil on Knighton. Soon, the citizens of Knighton would be serving Jestro, not laughing at him.

Jestro and The Book of Monsters launched their attack right away. With a wave of a magic staff over the pages of The Book of Monsters, evil monsters sprang to life.

A team of brave knights banded together to fight them. Clay Moorington and his friends Lance Richmond, Macy Halbert, Aaron Fox, and Axl took up their shields and charged against the monsters. But muscle and iron are no match against magic monsters.

In the end, I was the only one who could stop them. I cast a powerful magic spell to destroy

the monsters and . . . *boom!* Jestro
and The Book of Monsters were blown
far away from the castle. Although
the monsters were defeated, my
library was also destroyed, and
dangerous Books of Evil were
scattered across the kingdom.

The explosion also left me
trapped as a digital hologram in
the castle's computer system. But
it isn't all bad. Now, I am able to
harness the power of magic and
technology together. In this new
form I can download magical NEXO
Powers to the knights, so they can
defeat whatever monsters attack.

Now it's a fair fight. Clay,
Lance, Macy, Aaron, and Axl train
with their NEXO Weapons and NEXO
Shields so they'll always be ready
when Jestro and The Book of
Monsters attack—and they will! The
NEXO KNIGHTS team has only just
begun to see what Jestro's monsters
can do . . .

CHAPTER 1

The sun was setting when the NEXO KNIGHTS team's rolling castle—the Fortrex—rumbled up to the village of Spittoon. The sky was awash in bright orange and pink streaks, making the village look peaceful and welcoming. But the knights of Avatron knew looks could be deceiving. There were dark powers at work in their usually peaceful land—specifically, Jestro, the court's former jester, and an ancient Book of Monsters. Jestro was using the book to release monsters all over the kingdom. So these five new graduates of the Knights'

Academy were on a quest to try to bring peace and safety back to the Realm of Knighton.

"I sense a great power near the rough-and-tumble town of Spittoon," said Merlok 2.0 from inside his operating system. Once a powerful wizard (with a seriously snazzy wizard's beard, hat, swishy cloak, and the rest of the look), Merlok had recently gotten sucked into a computer. Now, he existed as a complicated computer program—with some pretty cool digi-magic at his disposal.

Merlok 2.0 was only just getting used to his new powers . . . and his new look. As part of the Fortrex's computer system, Merlok 2.0 was now a bright-orange hologram. With his digi-magic, he was able to help the NEXO KNIGHTS team when they most needed it. He could download NEXO Powers right into their armor. If they needed a specific kind of help during a battle, they could summon Merlok's help and—*ka-pow!*—instant digi-magic fighting powers!

Merlok 2.0 breathed deeply. Though he couldn't actually smell anything from inside his computerized shell, he knew deep breaths and a calm voice always made a person seem wiser. Deep breath in, deep sigh out. The digital wizard's voice rang out over the Fortrex's operating system as he scanned the village in front of their rolling castle. "I can feel the power surrounding Spittoon in my ancient bones."

Clay Moorington—the most knightly of all the NEXO KNIGHTS heroes—gazed out from the highest tower of the Fortrex. Clay adjusted his blue-and-gold armor and puffed out his chest. "Spittoon is the toughest village in the Realm," he told Merlok 2.0 and Lance Richmond, his fellow knight.

"They spit a lot," Lance noted casually. "It's unsanitary."

Clay ignored the useless information as he squinted out over the village of Spittoon. Lance never took things seriously enough for a true knight, and it frustrated Clay. The Knights' Code told Clay that he must consider their next move carefully. He wished he wasn't the only one in the group who worried about the impression he and the other knights were making on the people of the Realm. Because they had just graduated from the Knights' Academy, the five NEXO KNIGHTS heroes still had a long way to go before they had fully earned the trust and respect of the people of the Realm.

"We're gonna have to make an entrance that impresses them," Clay said. He had a feeling Lance would like this idea—handsome, popular Lance loved nothing more than to make a grand entrance. And because he was the most famous of the knights, Lance absolutely loved being noticed.

Clay turned and spoke to a group of mechanical Squirebots who were anxiously awaiting their orders. "Squires, play the 'Fanfare of Fortitude.'" On his command, the band of Squirebots—who called themselves The Boogie Knights—played a regal song. As the music washed over the valley, Clay turned to address the people of Spittoon. "Greetings, citizens of Spittoon! We are the Knights of Knighton, sworn protectors of the Realm."

The people who were gathered below looked up. For a moment, it almost seemed like they were cowering in fear. Then it was clear that they _were_ cowering in fear. At the sound of Clay's voice, many of Spittoon's villagers scattered and ran for cover. Inside their homes, the citizens shuttered their windows and doors.

"They seem a bit, um . . . skittish," Merlock 2.0 said.

Lance yawned, then shot Clay an amused smile. "See? You scared them with your boringness, Clay."

"This is supposed to be the toughest village in the Realm?" Clay scoffed.

"Times change," Lance told him. He shrugged arrogantly and added, "You gotta change with them." He nodded at the musical Squirebots. Wiggling his eyebrows, he ordered, "Put a little funk in that fanfare, will ya?"

The Boogie Knights cranked up the funk factor. The band of robots danced and swayed as they blasted their trumpets and lutes.

"Lance," Clay growled. This was not a time for nonsense! "What are you doing?"

Lance shrugged. He knew it would all work out—eventually. When you were Lance, things always did. "I'm working on our entrance, Clay-man. You only get one chance to make a first impression, you know."

"Yes, I do." Clay held out his hand to silence The Boogie Knights' trumpet section. "Which is why I hoped—as per our Knights' Code—we would present ourselves with power, respect, and solemn dignity."

Aaron Fox burst out onto the balcony just in time to add, "And no fear!" The most daring of the knights zoomed past the others. Aaron often used his shield as a hoverboard, which really ruffled Clay's armor

(Clay wished his fellow knight would realize his shield was *not* a toy!).

With a twist and a backflip, Aaron leapt onto his hover shield and dropped off the side of the balcony tower. Whooping, Aaron blasted away from the Fortrex and soared toward the houses that lined the quiet streets of Spittoon. His snazzy green-and-gray armor was a streak of color in the darkening sky.

As Aaron raced toward the village, the town roared to life. Many of the villagers who hadn't already hidden away inside their homes screamed and ducked for cover. Aaron zoomed over the tops of houses, his hover shield skimming across rooftops before it delivered him into the center of the village.

Clay watched the mayhem from above. Suddenly, he realized Aaron wasn't the only one of the knights who had ventured out into Spittoon. Axl, the largest—and hungriest—of the knights had also made his way into the town's center. The enormous knight lumbered through the town like a gentle giant, but the villagers ran from him like he was an ogre! Clay watched him from above, then called out, "Axl!"

But Axl was too distracted by a food cart. As Clay watched on from the Fortrex, Axl grabbed a chunk of meat from the vendor's stand. "Boring?" Axl grunted, drooling over the meat. "BOAR-ing!" He gobbled up the chunk of boar in one bite, hardly noticing that the shopkeeper had jumped up and fled when he saw Axl coming. "Yum!" Axl said happily, munching loudly.

"Why are they all so afraid of everything?" Clay wondered aloud as the people of

Spittoon scattered. "They should be spitting and grunting and scratching themselves, if memory serves. What do you think, Merlok? Lance?" He turned. Neither the wizard nor Lance was on the balcony with him any- more. "Merlok? Lance?!" Clay peered over the tower wall again.

In town, Lance had managed to find a pack of Squirazzi and a few adoring fans. Lance posed and preened, waiting for the usual happy screams. He *loved* being such a popular guy. Lance blew air kisses at the crowd, waving majestically. But instead of cheering and clapping, the crowds around him fled. They screamed with terror.

"Wow," Lance said, brushing his hair away from his face. "Something really is weird here."

Clay looked around, realizing he was alone—with only The Boogie Knights for backup—at the top of the tower. He shrugged at the band and said, "You might as well go down there, too. Just as long as you take—" But before he could finish his orders, the Squirebots leaped over the edge of the wall and slid into Spittoon. Clay sighed. ". . . As long as you take the stairs."

The Boogie Knights crashed at the bottom, landing in a tumbled heap of instruments. Clay was furious. Why was he the only one who took this job seriously?! "Does anybody remember our plan to make a 'respectful, dignified' entrance?"

"I do, Clay," said Macy Halbert. She strutted out onto the balcony and gazed out over Spittoon. As the king's daughter, Macy understood the words respectful and dignified better than anyone . . . she just didn't *enjoy* being respectful and dignified when it meant she couldn't also be rough and tumble. Macy wanted nothing more than to have some fierce fun once in a while! "Watch this—and this!" Macy swung her mace around her head, pretending she was deep in battle. Her red ponytail swung through the air as she whipped her powerful weapon around and around. "And some of this!" Macy grunted and swung, eager to impress her fellow knight with her toughness.

"All I can say is . . ." Clay broke off suddenly. "Oh no!" Below them, a small child was standing on the edge of a well. She had her arms outstretched, trying to grab a balloon that had escaped from her chubby fingers. The hairs on the back of Clay's neck stood up. It looked like a citizen was in danger— and that meant it was time for a real hero to take action! With a powerful jump, Clay leapt over the edge of the castle wall and slid into the village. He whisked the child out of harm's way just before she toppled into the well.

"Now *that* was awesome!" Aaron cheered. He leaned against his hover shield and cheered. "What's Lance talkin' about? You *totally* know how to make an entrance, Clay!"

"I wasn't 'making an entrance,'" Clay huffed. "I was saving this young damsel in distress." He smiled down at the little girl, patting her head gently. "Now run along, little girl. Oh . . . and don't forget your balloon!" He held out the girl's balloon, expecting her to thank him with a grateful smile.

But instead, the girl's mother rushed forward and grabbed her daughter away from the pack of gathered knights. "My baby!" she screeched. "My baby! My baby!"

As the mother and child raced away from the knights, Aaron shrugged one shoulder. Then he reached forward and popped the balloon with a cheeky grin. The few remaining villagers who hadn't yet gone into hiding screamed when they heard the sound of the popping balloon. Then they fled, too. Within seconds, the entire town center was deserted. The knights were alone.

Clay was totally stumped. He couldn't understand why everyone in the town was running from them in fear. Turning to his fellow knights, Clay asked, "*What* is going on here?!"

The five knights returned to the Fortrex Command Center to discuss the situation with Merlok 2.0. The team's two knights-in-training, Ava and Robin, joined them. Ava and Robin were on a break from their first year at the Knights' Academy. The two junior knights helped the team with tech and computer support when they were out on their missions, hoping someday they would get to join the NEXO KNIGHTS team, too.

The hologram of Merlok 2.0 spoke to all of them all in a serious voice, "Sorcery is going on here."

The knights gazed into their view-screen image of the village. The streets were all still empty, except for one lone villager who was peeking out his front door. When Axl burped—loudly, so it echoed through the valley—the villager jumped and slammed his door closed again.

"So much for a tough town," Lance said, rolling his eyes.

Ava punched a few buttons on the computer, pulling up a screen with a bunch of graphs. "Whoa," she murmured, her eyes flickering across the screen. "Some of these readings are off the chart. What's going on?"

"It's just as I suspected," Merlok 2.0 said ominously. "There is a Book of Magic. Somewhere in the Dark Woods. It is very powerful. And *very* scary. We need to get this evil book away from the village . . . or Spittoon will be lost to fear forever."

CHAPTER 2

eep in the Dark Woods, Jestro—the King's seriously unfunny court jester—was plotting with his new-found evil mentor: The Book of Monsters. Now, The Book of Monsters was no ordinary book. It could talk (too much, Jestro thought), scheme (very well, Jestro admitted), and was filled with dark, magical power. With the right spell, the caster could make evil creatures from the book's pages come to life.

But the knights had already defeated Jestro and the book's monsters before. The villains needed to make their monsters stronger, and there was only one way to do that. They had to find the eleven powerful Books of Dark Magic scattered across the Realm and feed them to The Book of Monsters. By eating the magical books, The Book of Monsters would become even more power-ful and release some extra-special creeps.

Now, in the Dark Woods, Jestro had stum-bled across a new book. And this one looked deliciously sinister.

"Watch it, clown-boy," The Book of Monsters warned as Jestro poked at the mysterious, glowing book with two sticks. "You gotta be very careful. You *don't* want to touch . . . *The Book of Fear*!"

"Yeah, yeah," Jestro muttered. He fur-rowed his brow as he tried to lift The Book of Fear to get a better look. The jester's painted-on smiley face looked shadowy and cruel in the dark forest. "So it's a spooky book. All I care about is that we beat those goody knights to it." He thrust the creepy book at The Book of Monsters, urging it to gobble it up. "Just open wide and . . . down the hatch."

The Book of Monsters sputtered, "Hey, wait . . . hold—" But Jestro had already shoved The Book of Fear into its mouth. The Book of Monsters chewed it up. Jestro laughed and waved his staff over The Book of Monsters' open pages. "Let's see what kind of monsters this gets us!"

The Book of Monsters burped. Purple smoke filled the air as The Book of Monsters shuddered and glowed. A moment later, three glowing Globlins popped out of The Book of Monsters' pages. All three of the evil flaming-red balls sprouted spider legs, then scurried around the dark forest.

They were ready to work their magic fear-power.

The Book of Monsters continued to shake and glow. More purple smoke filled the air. Then a moment later, another ominous creature popped out of the book's pages. She was tall and glowed like hot coals, with a long serpent's tail that slithered across the forest floor. The creature hissed, then flicked a pair of fiery whips into the air. Jestro had never seen anything like her before. She was so terrifying that he took a cautious step backward and hid behind a giant rock.

"Hey, scaredy-pants," The Book of Monsters teased Jestro. "Don't worry about Whiparella here. As long as her whips don't touch you, you'll be fine." Whiparella snapped her shimmering whips all around, narrowly missing Jestro's clownish face.

Jestro shrieked in fear, then tried to act cool about it.

"And that hair!" The Book of Monsters said, gazing at Whiparella. "Love it! Isn't she frightening?"

"Uh, yeah," Jestro agreed. "She's plenty scary. Not to me, obviously, but I can see how she would fill others with fear." He grinned mischievously. He had been looking for just the right creature to torture the NEXO KNIGHTS team. Giggling, Jestro said, "Like those pesky knights! Finally, they will know real fear!"

Nearby, the NEXO KNIGHTS team forged into the Dark Woods on their new quest. They were on the hunt for the powerful book Merlok 2.0 had warned them about. They had no idea Jestro had already found it and summoned some seriously frightful monsters.

"Hey," Macy said, glancing around at the creepy trees surrounding them. Rocks cast shadows over the dark ground, and branches drooped close over their heads. "Do you think we should wait until morning to look for this book?"

"You heard Merlok," Clay said. "We've got to get that thing before Jestro does."

"Why do you wanna wait, Macy?" Aaron teased. "Are you scared?" Aaron and the three other guys chuckled.

Macy scoffed, "No, I'm not *scared*. I just think it would be easier to see in the *Dark* Woods when it's *light* out."

"She sounds scared to me," Lance noted. The other three laughed again.

"Fear not, Macy," Clay said nobly. "There is nothing out here that can frighten us."

In the dark and gloomy forest, none of the knights noticed that Whiparella had slipped out of the shadows. Slowly, quietly, she crept past the knights. Then, with a quick flick of her wrist, she shot one of her whips out and grabbed Clay around the ankle. Tugging with a silent stealth, she pulled him into the forest with her.

"Clay!" Macy shouted when she realized their friend was gone. The four remaining knights skidded to a stop and spun around, searching through the shadows for some sign of Clay. But just like Macy had told them all, it was too dark.

Clay was nowhere to be seen.

"What happened?" Clay moaned when he came to a few minutes later. His eyes were glassy as he gazed into the thick forest. He blinked, unable to clear away all of the magical purple haze that clouded his vision. "Feels like something stung me . . ."

Whiparella smirked from the trees while she watched her magic take hold. Whenever her whips touched someone, that person was overcome with his or her own worst nightmares. Whiparella could figure out her victims' biggest fears and bring them to life! She was cooking up something truly fun for Clay . . .

Clay's eyes focused on the forest around him. He blinked. Then again, finally clearing the purple haze away. He looked into the trees, sure he had seen something strange. Was that—?

"Help!" A woman cried from nearby. As Clay watched, the woman was snatched up and carried away through the forest by a monster! From atop the monster's shoulders, the woman screeched in fear.

Clay leapt to his feet. It was time for him to take action! "Fear not, ma'am! I, Clay Moorington, Knight of Knighton, shall assist you in this dark wood!" He puffed out his chest. He flexed his biceps. He brushed off his armor. He did everything he could to make himself look as knightly as a true knight should.

The damsel rolled her eyes. "Will you just hurry up and save me already? This damsel is in some serious distress!"

Clay charged into the forest—and farther away from the rest of the knights. When there was a damsel to rescue, *nothing* could stand in his way. He raced through the forest, ducking under branches.

"Hurry, brave knight!" The damsel called out. "My captor is getting weary! It shall be with great ease that you do your knight's duty and rescue me now."

"For Justice!" Clay bellowed. "For Honor! For a damsel!" He raced forward. "There, m'lady! The monster has . . . gotten away?" He scratched his head and looked around. There was no sign of the damsel in distress *or* her captor. How had they escaped him?

A cry came from deeper in the forest. "Help!"

Clay was stumped. He had *never* failed in a rescue mission. And he certainly wasn't about to now. He scratched his chin, perplexed.

Nearby, Jestro and The Book of Monsters watched Clay with great delight. They knew that with Whiparella's magic at work, Clay would *never* save this damsel. And it was going to be great fun to watch his torture. "Oh, yeah!" The Book of Monsters said, laughing. "She found his fear!"

CHAPTER 3

Is it time to eat yet?" Axl asked, sniffing a stick to see if it smelled like food. The enormous knight poked under a large leaf, looking for any sign of Clay . . . and snacks.

Aaron groaned. "You just had third breakfast."

"Sorry, Axl," Lance told him. "First we find Clay, then we break for, um, first lunch." He headed off into the forest.

Macy called after him, "But I heard something over here." She pointed in the opposite direction.

"Perhaps we should split up," Lance suggested.

"In the Dark Woods?" Macy gasped.

"What . . . are you scared?" Aaron teased.

Macy shook her head. "No, of course not. I'm just saying we should, uh . . . split up and find Clay."

"Great idea," Lance muttered. "Wish *I'd* thought of that."

The knights all set off in different directions. After walking only a short distance, Axl tipped his head up and sniffed. His nose had caught a whiff of something delicious. But a moment later, Whiparella's whip hit him and Axl was overtaken with The Book of Fear's powers. His eyes glowed purple as the magic set in. "*Mmm.* Something smells good."

He had no idea Whiparella was lurking in

the bushes nearby, and that what he smelled was all just a trick to torture him . . .

Axl followed his nose to a large dinner table that was heaped with food and drinks in the middle of the forest. "So much food!" Axl grunted, his mouth watering. He rushed toward the table, ready to chow down. But just before he got to it, a gang of flaming Globlins shot out of the woods and devoured every last scrap of food on the table. There was nothing left but dirty dishes. It was Axl's worst nightmare—no food! "Noooooo!" he screamed.

Nearby, Jestro and The Book of Monsters watched the scene with great delight. Jestro giggled. "What a big fraidy cat," he said.

Elsewhere in the woods, Lance strutted proudly. He whistled and kept his shoulders back. He hoped that by trying to look relaxed, he might begin to feel a bit less tense, too. He peeked between two leaves—and got a brief glimpse of Whiparella's glowing whips. He scratched his head, curious about what he had seen . . .

But before he could figure it out, Whiparella snapped her whips at him. She was eager to overpower Lance with her cruel magic. He was hit. Lance swooned.

"Hey, bugs," Lance called out, feeling woozy as Whiparella's magic seeped into him. "Don't bite me . . . I'm a Richmond!" He spun around, but Whiparella had already slipped away, sight unseen. Lance's eyes went fuzzy and glowed purple with the book's magic.

Then a moment later, he brightened. Ahead of him in the forest he spotted Burnzie the monster. The enormous red beast was surrounded by a pack of Squirazzi! The Squirazzi's cameras were flashing like crazy, taking picture after picture of the big, foolish monster. Burnzie grinned and the monster's grotesque teeth glowed white with each flash of the camera.

"Hey!" Lance called out. Cameras always *loved* him. This would be the perfect opportunity for the Squirazzi to catch Lance acting like a true hero. His bravery would be captured on film, and he would be even *more* of a star than he already was! He would certainly be known from now on as the most *famous*, most *brave* knight in all the Realm. "Hey, vile monster! I shall set these noble Squirazzis free." He beamed at the cameras. "Free to take my picture for their celebrity photo spreads, that is!"

Lance lunged forward, striking blow after blow at Burnzie. "Action!" he cried out, naming each pose as he grinned for the cameras. "Glamour! Boy next door!" He raised his lance heroically. "Cover shot!"

After a short fight, Burnzie ran away defeated. Lance spun around, eager to smile and pose for the adoring Squirazzi cameras. But the strangest thing happened: None of them seemed the least bit interested in Lance.

In fact, rather than thanking him, one of the camera guys shouted at Lance. "Hey! You chased off Burnzie, the biggest celebrity in Knighton!"

"*What?*" Lance said, gaping at the Squirazzi. "He's a monster! And I just rescued you! And I'm a *celebrity*!"

"Uh-oh," the camera guy said, rolling his eyes at the other Squirazzi. "Poser alert.

Maybe we can still catch Burnzie!" He and the others began to run after the monster.

Lance chased after them. "Hold on! Perhaps you missed this look—I call it ... *Superstar!*" The forest around him seemed to glow as Lance gave them his most spectacular pose. But no one paid him any attention. Lance was growing desperate and terrified. What if he was—*gulp!*—not popular anymore? How could the cameras prefer ugly old Burnzie to *Lance Richmond*? "Hey, come back! I'll give you some shots from my good side!"

On the other side of the forest, Macy trudged through the dense woods. Suddenly, she, too, was hit by Whiparella's whip. Her eyes turned purple as the magic from The Book of Fear seeped into her body. "Hey!" She raised her mace, ready to fight back. Through the trees, the only thing she could see was a huge, glowing red monster. Macy recognized the monster right away. It was Sparkks! The knights had defeated Sparkks many times, and Macy knew she could take the ugly, one-eyed beast down easily. This would be a great chance to show the other knights that she really had what it took to be a hero! "Don't move, monster."

"Or what?" Sparkks hissed. "Gonna hit me with your little flowers? Ooh! Maybe you'll blind me with your shiny dress."

"What?" Macy blurted out. She glanced quickly at her weapon, gasping when she noticed it had turned into a bouquet of flowers! She reached up to touch her helmet, then realized it was no longer on her head. "Hey! Where's my mace? And my NEXO KNIGHTS helmet?"

"A knight?" Sparkks scoffed. "Oh, please. You're no *knight*! You're just some pretty little princess out picking flowers."

Macy lunged for the monster. "Why you—ughh!" She stumbled. Looking down, she could see that her armor had become a *princess dress*! "A sparkly dress? Gah!" Macy swatted at the pale-blue dress covered in foofy bows and ribbons. What a nightmare! A fussy dress, no helmet, and a bouquet of stinky flowers? What kind of knight carried flowers? Taking another step, Macy stumbled on the hem of her dress and fell to the ground.

"Aw," Sparkks teased. "Did the pretty little princess fall down?"

Very near the place where Macy was trying to battle Sparkks, Clay was still chasing after the damsel in distress. "Gotcha!" he said, lunging toward the woman's captor. But instead of getting a hold on her, he landed empty-handed, flat on his face.

"What is with you?" The damsel shouted at him. "I thought you were a brave and noble knight!" She used a silly voice to copy Clay's earlier words. "*'For justice! For honor!'*" Muttering, she added, "More like ... for *nothing!*"

Clay grumbled under his breath. He ran toward the woman's captor one more time—but again, he missed both the monster and the damsel in distress completely. "This can't be happening!" he wheezed, falling to the ground.

Just then, Macy stumbled toward him. She tripped on her dress and cried out, "Ahhh!"

"Whoa . . . Macy?" Clay said, gaping at her. "What happened to you?"

Macy looked down at her gown. "Is it that bad?"

"Well, uh, no. I've just never seen you look so . . ." Clay trailed off.

"Pathetic?" Macy prompted.

"Elegant," Clay said.

"Now you're just mocking me," Macy frowned. She grunted and tore at the dress, trying to pry away the annoying costume.

Clay shook his head. "No! I mean, at least you haven't completely failed as a knight. Like me. I can't . . ." He drew in a ragged breath. "I can't even rescue a damsel in distress!"

"Let me help," Macy offered. "I'm as tough and fearless as ever!" She tried to charge forward, but her dress was wrapped too tightly around her legs and she tripped again. Kicking at the fabric, Macy howled, "Stupid dress!"

Things were bad for all of the knights. Lost in the woods, each of them was being tortured by Whiparella's cruel magic. She had poisoned four of them with their own worst nightmares—only Aaron had yet to be hit.

Axl stumbled through the forest, desperate to find food. "Finally!" he said when he came upon another heaping banquet table in a clearing. "Lunch!"

The enormous knight raced forward, nearly crashing into Lance. Lance was still chasing after the band of Squirazzi, who were obviously eager to get away from him.

"C'mon!" Lance pleaded with the photographers. "Just one picture! I'm Lance Richmond! Everyone loves me!"

"Sorry," one of the camera guys said, spinning around. "Never heard of you."

Lance stomped, throwing a teensy tantrum. "You are *so* fired when my dad reaches out to your boss!" Lance raced after the cameras again, barely even noticing Axl as he rushed past.

Axl wasn't bothered, though. He only had eyes for one thing: food! Lots of food. He had never been so hungry, and all he wanted was a tiny bite. He charged toward the tables full of treats, howling when Globlins—once again—beat him to it. They dove on top of a pie, munched on a turkey leg, and ate every last scrap of food before Axl could get any! "What? My food!" Unable to stand the torture any longer, Axl began to weep. Big, horrible sobs that rocked the forest around him. He gazed at the table full of munched-on apple cores and empty platters and cried for the food he could still smell.

Suddenly, the Squirazzi rushed into the clearing and snapped pictures of him weeping beside the table.

"Really?" Lance shrieked. "Empty plates rate pictures?!"

"Empty plates!" Axl sobbed.

Macy, Clay, Axl, and Lance were all utterly miserable. But farther off in the forest, Aaron was still happy and whistling. Little did he know, he was about to come face-to-face with Whiparella!

The glowing monster leaped out of the forest and snapped her whip at Aaron. But he spun around so quickly that he was able to grab her whip in his bare hand. "Hey!" he barked, narrowing his eyes at her. "What gives?"

Whiparella looked at him, shocked. No one had ever caught her before. It was time to come up with a Plan B. "Oh, uh...*this* is what gives!" Whiparella screamed as she began to grow. While Aaron watched from the forest floor, Whiparella grew bigger and bigger, until she was towering over him. "And now," she growled. "I will fill you with fear!"

CHAPTER 4

giant Whiparella loomed over Aaron, cracking her whips. "Does my huge, frightening self scare you, tiny knight?"

Aaron's eyes grew wide as he took in the sight of the enormous glowing beast. "Whoaaaaa," he marveled. "That is *sick*! Do it again. Do it again!"

"What?" Whiparella gasped. "You're not frightened?"

Aaron shook his head. "No way! That looks awesome!"

"Well, then," Whiparella said, considering her next move. "Perhaps you have a fear of heights!" She lashed her whip at the ground and wrapped it around Aaron's body. She lifted him up, up, up—above the treetops, into the clouds.

When he was high in the sky, Aaron hooted and howled. "Woo-hoooooo!" he cheered. Aaron *loved* the thrill of heights. He slipped out of Whiparella's whip-hold and hopped onto his hover shield. Tilting his board, he rode down Whiparella's enormous side, using her glowing body as a giant, monstrous skate park. "Whoa!" Aaron said when he hopped off at the bottom. "Mad props for the ride, Mullet Mary."

Whiparella shrunk back down to her usual size and glared at Aaron. "What did you say?" She patted her hair, feeling self-conscious.

"This is not a mullet! It's a Dread Lock! And let's see how brave you are now . . . around my creepy crawlies!" She waved her hand in the air, and several Globlins rushed toward Aaron. They sprouted spider legs and skittered around his body, hissing at him.

"I am so totally . . ." Aaron said, eyeing the Globlins warily, ". . . buggin' out!" He hopped on his hover shield again, zooming around the spider-Globlins. As he wound through the pack of critters, the Globlins' legs got all tangled up and they fell into a messy heap. The critters whimpered, helpless, while Aaron whooped with joy. "That is so *off da shield*, yo. What else ya got, Chili Pepper Pam?"

"What?" Whiparella yelled. "That is not my name, either!"

Aaron shrugged. "Whatevs, Hot Links Heidi."

Whiparella growled, her anger mounting with each new name Aaron came up with. People did *not* tease Whiparella! "I am Whiparella!" she howled, flicking her whips in the air. She bared her pointed, fang-like teeth at Aaron, fuming. "With one snap from my whip, I can find your deepest, darkest fear and bring it to life!"

Aaron chuckled. "No way, Whippenstein."

"Yes way!" Whiparella argued. "And it's *Whiparella*! I've crushed all your knight friends. Not with weapons. But with their own worst nightmares." She cackled as she thought about how she'd tortured Axl with delicious food that he couldn't have. "I preyed upon Axl's fear of hunger—the greatest meal, always just out of reach."

Whiparella went on. "Fear of obscurity," she raised her arms in the air, thinking of

Lance and how he had pleaded with the Squirazzi to take just one picture of him. "Lance is a spoiled boy in a world that doesn't even care he exists."

She laughed, thinking about how Macy had struggled to move in her futzy princess dress. "I played with Macy's fear of being a princess who shall *never* become a true knight."

And then there was Clay, who was so desperate to prove himself to be a hero. Whiparella cackled. "Clay is overcome by his fear of failing. Not just the damsel in distress I created, but he fears failing with your beloved Knights' Code as well."

Aaron nodded, as though he understood. He leaned back against a giant boulder, sucking down a soda. "Good times. Right, *Wimp-arella*?"

"Stop that!" Whiparella screeched. Her

yellow eyes glowed with fury. "And tell me why my fear magic has no effect on you? I've got no sense of any fear from you!"

"That's because I've got NO FEAR!" Aaron roared. He lifted his bow and strummed on it like it was a guitar, screaming out a rock beat. "None whatsoever. Woo-hoo!" He raised his arms and pumped his fists in the air.

"But that can't be," Whiparella hissed. "Everyone has fears. Some are just less obvious. How about these classics..." She whistled, summoning up more scary things. First, she conjured up a monster standing at a chalkboard. On Whiparella's cue, the creature raked its long, talon-like fingernails across the board. A horrible screeching noise echoed through the forest. Whiparella covered her ears—the sound was horrible!

But Aaron loved it. "Ooh! Lemme play some harmony!" He pulled out his bow-guitar and jammed along with the music of the nails on the chalkboard.

Whiparella frowned. Then she got another idea. "Paging Doctor Sparkks, DDS." She grinned. "Everyone fears the dentist!" She shoved Aaron into a huge dentist chair, cackling as the dentist hovered over him with a whizzing dental drill.

"Woo!" Aaron cheered from inside his seat. "Nothin' to fear. I got *no* cavities. I'm a big brusher, yo. 'Cause plaque is whack!" He opened his mouth wide, letting the dentist have at him.

Whiparella was growing more and more frustrated with each failed attempt. "*Hmm. Ha!* The naked truth! That never fails to destroy you!" With a quick flip of her hand,

Whiparella zapped the clothes and armor right off Aaron's body.

Holding his shield in front of himself, Aaron glanced around the forest nervously. "Whoa, where did my armor go?"

Whiparella laughed. "You're completely exposed for all the world to see. Nowhere to hide now. Within moments you'll be—"

Aaron strutted proudly through the clearing. He announced, "I'm rockin' the commando look!"

"What?!" Whiparella growled.

"I've never felt so free!" Aaron told her. "Thanks, Whipper-Snapper."

Whiparella howled. She was *furious*! And she was also out of ideas. Furious, she stormed off to plot her revenge.

Aaron had stopped Whiparella from capturing him, but he still needed help to save his friends. *If only there was a NEXO Power that could make the other knights, um, unafraid . . .*

As if in answer to Aaron's thoughts, he heard Merlok 2.0's voice through his shield. "Prepare for NEXO Scan!"

This was exactly what Aaron needed! He raised his shield in excitement. "NEXOOOOO Knight!" he called.

"NEXO Power: Lion of Bravery!" Merlok 2.0 announced.

A moment later, Aaron's shield surged with new power as the NEXO Power downloaded. Aaron lifted his shield, sending beams of white, magical light out into the dark forest. Then he raced through the woods. It was time to save his friends from their worst nightmares!

earby, Clay had grown weak with the effort of trying to rescue the damsel in distress. He crawled through the forest, trying to catch the woman and her captor. Macy followed close behind.

"Please, monster," he begged, gasping for breath. The monster raced in circles around him, the woman clutching the monsters shoulders so she wouldn't fall off. Clay reached out to them, begging, "Stop . . . I must save the damsel. Or else . . . my honor, my chivalry . . . all that matters." His voice broke. "I have failed."

Aaron burst out of the woods at that moment. Waving his shield proudly, he cried, "You talkin' about *this* damsel?" He shot two arrows—one at the monster, and one at the damsel in distress. The monster dissolved the moment the arrow struck.

While Clay watched, horrified, the woman hissed . . . and then she, too, morphed into a monster! She had been a creature disguised by Whiparella's powers all along. Aaron shot another arrow at the creature, then whooped when it dissolved. "Boo-ya!"

"Aaron?" Clay said, looking from the two monsters to his fellow knight. "What are you doing here?" His eyes bulged out of his head, then he looked down, embarrassed. "And where's your armor?"

Aaron glanced down at his still-naked body. With a casual shrug, he explained, "Ah, some whip lady took 'em. I think she was try-ing to scare me."

"Well, uh," Clay cringed. "Honestly, your lack of modesty is scaring me a bit."

Aaron grinned. "Oh . . . sorry. Be right back." He dashed through the woods, return-ing a moment later wearing a full set of green-and-gray armor.

"Aaron," Clay asked. "Tell us more about this 'whip lady'?"

"Oh," Aaron said. "Well, she snaps you with her whip and your worst fears come to life."

"What?" Macy asked. Everything that had happened in the woods was suddenly start-ing to make more sense.

Aaron proudly added, "But I have no fear! Woo-hoo! So it was just kinda fun for me."

"We must find the others," Clay told Aaron and Macy. "But . . . the fear."

Aaron shook his head. "Hey, no sweat, bro. You still probably got her scary magic in ya. No worries. I'll take the lead."

Clay nodded gratefully, then he and Macy followed Aaron deeper into the forest. By the time they reached Axl, the huge knight was completely exhausted—and starving.

"So hungry," he moaned. He grabbed for another drumstick on the table. But a Globlin got hold of it at the same time and the creature and Axl played tug-of-war with the chunk of meat. "Please," Axl begged, his body collapsing from hunger. "One bite . . ."

Suddenly, one of Aaron's arrows zipped into the clearing. When it struck the drumstick, the meat dissolved into nothing. Aaron soared into the clearing on his hover shield and batted at the Globlins with his bow. The little monsters scattered. One by one, Aaron hit each of them with arrows and the creatures turned into dust.

Now, the only one left to save was Lance. As Aaron, Axl, Macy, and Clay came upon their famous friend in the forest, they could hear him begging. "C'mon," Lance pleaded with the Squirazzi. "Please! I'm Knighton's most celebrated celebutante."

"What'd you say your name was?" one of the photographers asked.

"Lance! Lance Richmond!"

"Oh," the Squirazzi said. "Yeah, never heard of you."

Before Lance could respond, Axl came crashing through the trees. Aaron released one of his arrows, and the first Squirazzi disappeared in a *poof*! One by one, the rest followed. Lance grabbed one of their cameras and took pictures as his fellow knights bashed the magical monsters. The camera flashed just as one of the Globlins was conked over the head. Lance cheered, "Now *that's* what I call a 'cover shot!'"

While the knights celebrated their victory, Whiparella returned to Jestro and The Book of Monsters to await further instructions. She told Jestro about her encounter with Aaron, feeling embarrassed that she had failed. She hung her head as she told him how she had failed—all thanks to Aaron.

"What do you mean he had 'no fear?'" Jestro wailed.

"Every one of them crumbled before the terror of their own worst nightmares," Whiparella told him. She lowered her voice to add, "Except the archer. My magic didn't work. He was afraid of *nothing*."

Jestro spun around and screamed at The Book of Monsters. "Are you kidding me? I thought you said she could scare anyone?"

The Book of Monsters asked, "Did you try the creepy crawlers?"

Whiparella nodded.

"What about the dentist?" The Book of Monsters said.

Whiparella nodded again. Sulking, she said, "I even gave him an 'out-of-clothes experience.'"

The monsters gathered around in the forest all gasped. Sparkks asked, "Completely naked? In public?!"

"Yikes!" Sparkks yowled. "Talk about nightmares!"

The Book of Monsters grumbled, "Wow. I hate the dentist. But that didn't even faze him, huh?"

"No," Whiparella whined. "He called me all kinds of names, like 'Hot Links Heidi' and . . ." She sniffed. "'Wimp-arella.'"

The other monsters all gasped again. "Aww," Sparkks said sadly, patting her on the shoulder. "That's terrible."

The Scurrier who had spent the whole night torturing Clay chimed in, "It doesn't even make any sense!"

Burnzie shook his head. "You poor thing. Do you need a hug?"

Whiparella nodded gratefully, and all her monster pals squeezed her into a friendly hug.

The Book of Monsters whispered, "'Wimp-arella'? That's pretty good."

Jestro growled at the book and the creatures. "Stop that! All of you, stop that! There will be none of that while I'm here! *No hugging* until we stop those knights! That Aaron must have *something* he's scared of."

"Yeah," came a voice from the woods. It was Aaron! He added, "I'm scared of your terrible comedy routines, Jestro."

Jestro turned just in time to see the knights marching toward him, ready for battle. Jestro shouted, "Now's your chance, Whiparella! Hit him with everything you've got!"

Whiparella looked up from the hug. Her eyes narrowed. She flicked her whips. Then she hissed, "Yes! I don't believe *anyone* fears nothing!" Her whips glowed with magic as she swung both of them at Aaron. She put all her strength into the attack.

But Aaron was ready. He fired back with two arrows. Each one hit one of her whips, sending them backward—straight toward Jestro!

With a *smack*, they hit the evil court jester right in the face. Jestro frowned as the whips' magic sunk in. His eyes glowed. He wobbled and tried to focus on the forest around him. "Uh..." he asked, woozy. "Was that supposed to happen?"

"Whoa," The Book of Monsters gasped, cringing. "You were hit with double snaps! Things might get a little scary."

Jestro swayed as the magic took hold. He blinked, and when his droopy eyes opened again, he was back in the Joustdome at the castle. He was on stage, performing for everyone. "Wait," he mumbled aloud. He wasn't sure if he was in the forest or the castle. It was the most real dream he'd ever had! "Where am I?"

The Book of Monsters told him, "Don't worry: you're just in the middle of a very severe fear-dream."

Jestro could hear The Book of Monsters speaking to him, but the voice sounded far away. He looked around the Joustdome, staring nervously up into the stands filled with jeering crowds. He muttered, "But . . . but, I'm in the Joustdome. The last time I looked like a fool. And there are knights here, too. Aaron . . ." He blinked and swayed. "Oh, I get it! Aaron said the only thing he feared was my terrible comedy routine. So now . . . I shall destroy him!" He stood up and lunged for Aaron. But suddenly, the only thing he could see was people—laughing at him. Everyone was making fun of him!

"Uh," The Book of Monsters told him. "Aaron was only joking about that before. This is actually *your* worst nightmare."

"It is?" Jestro whispered. He glanced around again. All he could see was a sea of faces, and they were all laughing at him.

In the dream, people were screaming, "This guy's awful!" and "He's the worst jester ever!"

Jestro covered his head. "No! This can't be happening. Not again…keep it together!" Suddenly, he was holding a sword, a mace, a halberd, and some arrows. While everyone watched, Jestro tried to juggle them—but they all just rained down around him. He spun plates on sticks, but they all crashed and broke on the Joustdome floor. "Nooooo!" Jestro moaned, then dropped to the ground. He closed his eyes, hoping to hide from the scene inside the nightmare.

The evil jester curled into a ball on the forest floor, his body twitching with fear. All of his monsters leaned over him, waiting for him to wake up from his nightmare.

"Uh . . ." Macy said, staring at Jestro wide-eyed. "Is he okay?"

The Book of Monsters gazed down at its master—then looked at the knights. "Yeah," the book said. "But now it's *my* worst fear. We've lost again." The Book of Monsters screamed at the other creatures. "Grab him! And let's scram!" Sparkks and Burnzie snatched Jestro off the forest floor. Then the book, all the monsters, and Jestro fled in fear.

By the next morning, everything had gone back to normal in the village of Spittoon. Now that The Book of Fear was gone, the knights were quickly able to restore order to the tough town. People were spitting and snarling at each other, just like the good old days. "Watch your step!" one guy screamed.

"Have a terrible day," yelled another.

When the Fortrex rolled out of town, the villagers waved their fists and spit and pushed one another around some more. It was life as usual in Spittoon—and the knights were off on their next adventure.

"I still think we should have chased after them and . . . *wham!*" Aaron said, slamming his fist into the palm of his hand. He couldn't believe they had let Jestro and The Book of Monsters get away without a fight!

Clay shook his head. "The Knights' Code says we're supposed to defend the down-trodden. Jestro seemed pretty down." He thought back to the previous night, cringing at the memory of his failed rescue. Even though it had all been a dream, it had been a *terrible* dream, and Clay couldn't stop thinking about how he had failed to save the damsel in distress. "But then, I utterly failed the whole 'Knights' Code' thing, didn't I?"

Macy patted him on the shoulder. "Aw, c'mon. Don't be so hard on yourself, Clay. We all fell for that slithery monster's tricks."

"Not Aaron," Clay said. "The Fear Monster looked for his deepest fear and all she found was *nothing*."

Merlok 2.0 cut in, "Ah, but sometimes 'nothing' is the greatest fear of all."

Clay looked stumped. "Sorry, Merlok 2.0, but that makes no sense. Aaron is the truest of knights."

"I suggest you read your *Knights' Code* again, Clay," said Merlok 2.0. "It says: 'We are many, we are one.'"

Macy nodded. "Yeah, and that means we're a team. We've each got our own strengths that make the team stronger. And it makes each of us stronger, too."

Clay considered this for a moment. He wasn't so sure he agreed.

But Macy went on, "The truest of knights—like *you*, Clay—should understand that."

Clay sighed. Sure, working as a team was important. But he also worried that he wasn't as tough as he ought to be. He was on a quest to be the best. "Yes, Macy," he said. "But I don't know. I still wish I was like Aaron— afraid of nothing!"

Merlok 2.0 raised his eyebrow. He stroked his beard. Suddenly, he had an idea. It was time to show the knights that *everyone* had a fear—you just had to find it. A moment later, the wizard's computerized hologram faded away. Then the castle slammed to a stop and all the power went out. Aaron crashed to the ground when even his hover shield pow- ered down.

"Hey," Aaron said from the floor. "What gives?"

Ava punched at buttons on the computer, trying to power everything back up. "Sorry," Ava said, shrugging. "Some kind of power surge. Merlok 2.0 is offline."

"Is he okay?" Clay asked, concerned.

"He's fine," Robin told the more experienced knights. "But we'll have to shut down everything in the castle to get him back up and running again."

"Even my shield?" Aaron said, a note of panic creeping into his voice.

"No choice," Robin shrugged. "We've gotta make sure there's no electrical interference while we reboot."

"Yeah," Ava agreed. "The system is very fragile. So stay completely silent and still during the reboot. Do *nothing*!"

"What?" Aaron shrieked. His body began to tremble. In a whisper, he asked, "But,

but . . . how am I supposed to stay still? How long will this take?"

Quietly, Robin told him, "According to this message from Merlok, it will take about ten minutes."

"I have to do *nothing*?!" Aaron screamed. "For a whole *ten minutes*?!" His eyes went wide, and he began to sweat. His body was shaking and trembling.

Lance cocked an eyebrow. "Everything okay, Aaron?"

Aaron shuddered. He was so overcome by the idea of doing nothing that he wasn't even able to speak. "Uhh," he moaned. His body began to twitch and his face was filled with terror. "Ugh . . . not moving. I can't take *nothing*! Ahhhhh!" He threw his arms up in the air and screamed. He ran from the room and the other knights were left to stare after him.

A moment later, the system roared to life again. The hologram of Merlok reappeared— and the wizard was smirking.

"What was *that* all about?" Clay asked.

"Oh," Merlok said, chuckling. "You just saw Aaron's greatest fear: when there is nothing to do. As The Fear Monster said, he is literally afraid of . . . *nothing*!"

"Really?" Macy said. It seemed so silly— and impossible.

"No one is completely fearless, Clay," Merlok said. "Not even the truest of knights."

Clay nodded, finally understanding. He grinned at their trusty wizard advisor. "Merlok . . . you didn't have anything to do with that system reboot, did you?"

The orange hologram of a wizard shrugged. "What? Me?" The corners of his mustache lifted in a smile. "Uh, no . . . I'm a wizard. Not a rebooting, techno-mathingy guy who just happened to bump into a few switches here and there that go beep beep boop."

Macy's mouth hung open. She lifted one eyebrow and whispered to Clay, "What is he talking about?"

Merlok 2.0 continued to make beeping sounds while the rest of the knights shook their heads, confused.

"I don't know," Clay said. "I'm afraid to ask. Very afraid."

Macy nodded and laughed. "We all are sometimes, aren't we?"

Macy and Clay exchanged a smile. Merlok 2.0 continued to *beep* and *boop*, while Axl settled in at a table to eat until he was stuffed. Lance brushed his hair and smiled at himself in the mirror. And Aaron hopped onto his hover shield and raced around the castle, relieved that he hadn't been forced to spend ten minutes doing nothing. The thought was far too terrifying!

As the Fortrex rolled on toward the knights' next adventure, it seemed that things were back to normal—for now. But even as they all relaxed into their favorite activities, the NEXO KNIGHTS team had no doubt their next quest would find them soon. And they would be ready. Separated and alone, the knights had given into their fears. But as a team they were strong enough to overcome any scary challenge. Together, they would restore harmony to the Realm and defeat Jestro and his monsters once and for all!